MOLLY MEETS
HER MATCH

This Large Print Book carries the
Seal of Approval of N.A.V.H.

MOLLY MEETS HER MATCH

Val Whisenand

Thorndike Press • Thorndike, Maine

Library of Congress Cataloging in Publication Data:

Whisenand, Val.
    Molly meets her match / Val Whisenand.
        p. cm.
    ISBN 1-56054-613-1 (alk. paper : lg. print)
    1. Large type books. I. Title.
[PS3573.H4436M6   1993]   92-40991
813'.54—dc20   CIP

All the characters in this book have no existence outside
the imagination of the author and have no relation
whatsoever to anyone bearing the same name or names.
They are not even distantly inspired by any individual
known or unknown to the author, and all incidents are
pure invention.

Thorndike Large Print® Candlelight Series edition
published in 1993 by arrangement with Harlequin
Enterprises B.V., Fribourg Branch.

Cover photo by Tom Knobloch.

The tree indicium is a trademark of Thorndike Press.

This book is printed on acid-free, high opacity paper. ∞

To the *real* dog and human heroes at
Canine Companions for Independence
P.O. Box 446
Santa Rosa, CA 95402
I wouldn't have believed such miracles
were possible
if I hadn't seen them with my own eyes

Chapter One

Molly Evans smiled over at the eager, black Labrador retriever wiggling on the car seat beside her. His enthusiasm was contagious.

"You're right, Fremont," she said. "We're almost there."

The dog began to try to shuffle in a circle, in spite of the seat belt fastened to his harness, and nearly toppled off onto the floor.

Molly laughed. "Easy, boy."

She stopped her Volkswagen van in the nearest open slot in the mall's parking lot, rolled up the windows and tucked stray wisps of hair back into the neat French braid at the back of her head as she got out.

Hurrying around the van, she opened the passenger door to check the straps that held the brightly-colored orange-and-green backpack to Fremont's body. As a puppy, his harness had needed constant adjustment to keep up with his rapidly increasing size, and although he wouldn't get much bigger, she still checked from habit.

His excited wriggling made an otherwise simple task difficult. No time like the present to remind him he had a job to do, she thought. Later, they'd play.

Molly took the youngster's face between her hands and stared into the deep chocolate of his eyes. "Fremont. Sit."

To her delight the furry black hips plopped obediently onto the car's seat. One rear leg hung off, but at least he was trying. She reacted immediately, fawning over him as if he had just won the Nobel Prize for his intelligence. "Good boy!" She ruffled his silky ears. "Oh, what a good boy!"

As usual, Fremont temporarily forgot he'd been commanded to sit and once again began to frisk with the joy of life and of having pleased a human.

Understanding the cause and effect of his actions, Molly gently corrected him, calmed him and finished adjusting the straps of his pack. It was filled with lightweight objects, balanced to give him less trouble, but heavy enough to remind him he was in training. The necessary seriousness regarding his work as a companion dog for the handicapped would come soon, now that he was nearly mature.

The trick was to develop an eager worker who loved helping his master or mistress, yet was trustworthy in all situations. No easy feat, Molly thought, which was one of the reasons she'd taken on the job of trainer. Life without challenge was too dull.

"I'll bet this trip isn't dull, the way you're feeling this morning, Fremont," she said lightly. "You'll see to that, won't you?"

Giving the dog the command to exit, she helped him jump safely to the ground. He looked up at her with such guileless, trusting eyes, Molly felt her own vision misting. This was the indefinable spark of something special that she always looked for in potential assistance dogs. Training a puppy like Fremont until he could be placed with the person he would assist for the rest of his life was what made her own life worth living.

The bright sunshine glistened off his ebony coat as Fremont waited patiently at Molly's feet. What a grand and glorious morning this is, she thought. Squinting into the morning sun, she started toward the mall, the dog trotting close to her side. What a pleasure to be alive!

Had Brian Forrester known the Escondido Mall would be so crowded he wouldn't have come. It was just that he'd finally grown so sick of the life he was now forced to lead that his frustration level had overridden his reticence.

Grumbling, he coasted out of the way of the jostling people and turned to watch them pass, annoyed at having to look up to do it. What a motley crew. Of course, this was Southern California, the home of casual with a capital *C*, but some of the outfits were actually humorous. Funny, he'd never really noticed things like that before.

Nor had he noticed how hard it was to get from one level of the three-story mall to the next. Escalators abounded. However there was only one elevator, as far as he could figure out, and it was halfway to hell and gone in the opposite direction.

"Good planning, Forrester," he muttered. Next time, if he ever did anything this dumb again, he'd have his brother, Sam, drop him off nearer to the elevator.

He checked his watch and was amazed to find he'd been at the mall for less than thirty minutes. Sam wasn't due back to pick him up for another couple of hours but at the rate he was making progress — or *not* making it — that would be barely enough time to buy the gifts he'd come for. He owed Sam and his wife plenty and it just didn't seem right to not personally reward them for their tolerance and forbearance. Alter all, hadn't Sam kept him on the company payroll when he wasn't good for much more than being a talking doorstop?

Brian shrugged. "Lousy attitude, Forrester," he mumbled. "You're alive, aren't you?"

"Yeah, I guess you could call it that," he replied with more than a little sarcasm. Reaching down, he gripped the outer rim of the wheels on his chair and pushed off into the crowd.

The first thing Molly noticed about the man was his thick, brown head of hair and the rippling muscles of his shoulders and arms. He was waiting ahead of her in line for the elevator and wearing one of those muscle shirts. In his case, the name fit. So did the shirt. *Very well.*

Finding herself blushing, Molly turned her attention toward Fremont to distract herself. The ploy didn't work. As the elevator doors opened and the man began to propel his wheelchair forward, she found she couldn't take her eyes off the sensuous, rippling movement of his broad back.

Others were staring at him, too, but obviously for far different reasons, while some folks dodged around the man as if he weren't even there. The behavior of the crowd was all too typical. Their exposure to individuals with handicaps had been minimal and they simply didn't know how to act. Molly pitied them for their ignorance.

The small elevator was suffocatingly crowded; so much so that the man had no room in which to pivot his chair for easy egress. His back remained toward Molly. Only by leaning away at an unnatural angle could she keep from inadvertently touching him or his chair.

Fremont had no such polite compunctions. He stuck his big, black nose into the space between the back of the chair and the man's arm and nuzzled him. With a start, the man craned his neck and looked behind him.

"Fremont! Oh, I'm so sor—" Molly froze in mid-sentence. The darkest blue eyes she had ever seen were scrutinizing her. Between thick eyebrows there were faint frown lines. On his lips was a scowl trying hard not to become a half smile.

"Yes?" he said.

The vibration of his voice tingled along Molly's nerve endings from the roots of her light brown hair to the soles of her canvas tennies. Suddenly she wished she'd worn nicer clothes. Jeans and a T-shirt were fine for work, but she felt tacky under the steady gaze of such an attractive man.

"Sorry," she said, lowering her eyes. She wasn't uneasy because of the man's physical problems. On the contrary, *she* was the one with the problem and found her reactions to him very unsettling.

The man's scowl deepened, and he quickly looked away. Molly knew from experience what he had to be thinking, and he was dead wrong. Not that she could blame him. Rejection by so-called "normal" members of society was a common reaction that the disabled often encountered. Because this particular man seemed to be taking it so personally, she deduced his affliction was fairly recent.

And she knew she had hurt his feelings. She'd glimpsed it in his eyes just before she'd acted the coward and looked away. He mustn't be allowed to continue thinking she was put off by his condition, whatever it was. Confessing to him would be difficult, but she saw no other way to correct his obvious misconceptions. Fair was fair. There was no need to go into embarrassing detail, but the man deserved to hear the truth — she found him attractive.

The elevator doors opened onto the third-floor landing. Molly stepped back, Fremont held in close check beside her, and let a mother with two young children rapidly disembark, then got off herself.

The man in the wheelchair was acting as if he, too, was in a hurry. Whirling the chair in a one hundred eighty degree arc, he propelled it quickly toward the door.

Molly waited for him, out of the way. The

elevator had halted several inches lower than the threshold, she noticed. For a person who could walk, that discrepancy posed no special problem. For the man in the wheel-chair, it could be a dangerous precipice.

She saw the determination in his eyes as he bumped the ledge and realized he wasn't going to be able to roll out easily. His jaw set; his eyes narrowed. He tried again. The chair's small front wheels caught on the lip of the threshold, giving him a jolt.

Three young people, two boys and a girl whom Molly hadn't noticed before, were trying to squeeze out the elevator door past the wheelchair and having no luck. The tallest, a thin youth wearing a leather vest and sporting an earring beneath long, stringy hair protested loudly. "Hey, man. Get it in gear, will you?"

His male companion joined in. "Yeah. Move it. Or we'll move it for ya."

The two boys reached for the back of the chair. Molly's latent anger surfaced. "Leave him alone," she ordered. Fremont stiffened at her tone, his senses heightened.

The boys stared. So did the man in the wheelchair.

"I'm Molly Evans," she said to him. "And this is Fremont."

"Brian Forrester," the man said. Giving his

left wheel a push, he jockeyed out of the way and let the three youths pass. He, however, was still a prisoner of the tiny elevator. Shoppers waiting to board were acting impatient.

"I have a friend who can jump his wheels up a curb," Molly said. "It's a matter of balance."

"I'm afraid I'm a little new at this," Brian replied. "And it makes me so damned mad, sometimes." He shrugged, giving up. "Want to lend me a hand?" To his surprise, Molly demurred.

"Nope. You can do it."

"What?"

"I said, you can do it. If you fall on your face, I'll pick you up." She paused, smiling. "Or Fremont will."

Making a disgusted face, Brian studied first Molly, then the ledge. "Great. I need an angel of mercy to rescue me, and instead I get some hard-nosed drill sergeant and a refugee from the dog pound."

"Flattery will get you nowhere. Have you ever maneuvered the front wheels up and over the leading edge of a thick carpet or rug?"

"Sure."

"Well, it's almost the same. Just higher. Make sure you're lined up straight, then go ahead."

"Just like that?" Brian scowled at her.

15

"Just like that." Waiting with every muscle in her body tensed to leap to his rescue if he miscalculated and went over backward, Molly smiled at him with feigned nonchalance. He needed help, all right, but not the physical kind. Brian Forrester needed confidence in his own abilities. Coddling him wouldn't give him that.

Brian's strong arms pushed forward. As he approached the ledge at a right angle, he leaned back enough to lighten the load on the front casters. They caught below the lip, shuddered once, then slipped over and out. The larger rear wheels followed easily. Everyone but Molly was looking away, embarrassed either by him or for him.

He came to a halt at her feet, ignoring everyone else. "Thanks."

She shook her head. "You'd have figured it out. You could have gotten out by backing up, too. Actually, that might have been easier."

"How'd you get to be such an expert? From your friend?" He turned parallel to her as she began to walk and they moved along together as naturally as if they'd done so often.

"It's my job," Molly said. She nodded at Fremont. "I train service dogs for the disabled — only I *hate* that word, don't you?"

"Disabled?" He snorted derisively. "Yeah,

I guess so. Haven't given it much thought, really. This is all pretty new to me."

"How did you get hurt?"

"Auto accident. I build — used to build special cars. Replicas. One day I was testing one of them and *wham*."

"No seat belt?"

"Hadn't installed it yet."

"Oh." Molly considered her next question carefully before asking it. "So what do you do now?"

"I'm a professional doorstop," Brian quipped, his voice dripping undisguised cynicism. He looked up at her and couldn't help but chuckle at her distressed expression. "Actually, I work for my brother, Sam."

"Doing what?"

"Thinking," he said slowly. "At least mostly. I used to be a pretty fair mechanic."

"Why don't you go back to doing that?" She saw his jaw muscles tense.

"What makes you think I haven't tried?" His resentment and frustration were more evident than he'd intended, and he quickly rationalized the reaction by reminding himself no one had the right to ask him such questions.

"Have you?" Molly pressed.

Now she'd really gone too far. "No. Not that it's any of your business."

Molly wanted to say, "That's what I figured," but kept those thoughts to herself. Instead, she held up her hands, palms toward him. "Okay. Simmer down. Think about this for a minute, will you? If we'd met under other circumstances, ones where you were on your feet instead of in that chair, what kinds of questions might we have asked and answered in the normal course of conversation?"

Brian hated to admit it, but she had a valid point. The logic of her argument made him thoroughly ashamed of his earlier response. He nodded, a wry half smile lifting one corner of his mouth. "You mean besides, 'Do you come here often?' and 'What's your sign?' "

"Exactly." She could see he was chagrined, and she sought to lighten the mood. "So, do you come here often?" The raising of her eyebrows twice in rapid succession added the perfect comic touch.

He laughed and shook his head. "No. I hate shopping, but I'm on a special quest, or I was. What brings you and the black avenger to the big city?"

"Training. For *him*, not me," she added with a broad grin.

Brian looked quickly from the dog to Molly's sparkling hazel eyes and made a snap decision. "So why don't you tag along with me. That is, if you don't think I'll spoil your lessons."

"Not at all." She smiled down as Brian reached out to ruffle the Labrador's ears the same way she often did.

"Just explain what you want me to do and I'm game," he said.

"Be yourself."

Brian made a face at her. "If I could be myself, I wouldn't be cruising around in this damn thing, that's for sure. I mean, how can I behave that will help old Fremont here?"

Molly shook her head. "I have plenty of spare wheelchairs and eager assistants at the school. He's quite used to people on wheels. Just go on about your business and we'll keep you company. Now, what are we shopping for?"

Brian regarded her seriously. "You're positive you don't mind? I'd hate to take up your time."

"Forget it. Consider yourself a training volunteer. We have lots of those at Faithful Friends, Inc."

"That's the name of the outfit you're with?"

"Uh-huh." She started to walk slowly.

He smiled, wheeling along beside her. "You know you're the first person I've met since my accident who's treated me like a fellow human being. It's damned refreshing."

19

Blushing, Molly couldn't help but smile, too.

"Except in the elevator when we first met," he added. "Then you acted like all the rest and ignored me the same way they did."

"No, I didn't. If I'd been able to really ignore you, I wouldn't have felt so embarrassed."

Reaching out, he took hold of Fremont's leash just below Molly's hand and stopped their forward progress. "Explain."

Well, here it was, she reasoned, her big chance to make things right and give him a needed ego boost. The trouble was, it was darned awkward to put it into words. The way their conversation had been progressing, she'd thought she'd get away without baring her soul. That, apparently, was not to be.

Molly cleared her throat. "Umm, I thought you'd caught me ogling your muscles," she said quietly. A deeper crimson flush stole up her cheeks.

"Were you . . . ?" His voice rose questioningly.

With a shrug, she nodded. " 'Fraid so. Those are some biceps you've got there. I'm only human." She waited, watching his astonished look fade.

"You're serious," Brian said, peering up at her.

For once Molly was glad she blushed easily. It gave credence to her confession.

His laugh started softly, with a shaking of his head. The happy noise increased in volume until passersby were staring. Tears moistened his eyes, and he grabbed his sides, rocking back and forth. "You were making a pass at me back there?" he finally choked out.

"Of course not. Not exactly, anyway. And you needn't be so crude about it." Suddenly truly mortified, Molly wished she were somewhere else, anywhere else but there, listening to his laughter. Not that she blamed him. Her clothes were clean but faded, her T-shirt said something about saving the environment and she couldn't even remember if she'd put on lipstick that morning. No wonder he found her confession funny rather than gratifying.

She pulled away from him, starting down the mall.

"Wait. Molly, wait!"

She didn't turn or look back, but Fremont did. His leash tangled around her ankles, bringing her to a staggering halt. By the time she'd freed herself, Brian had caught up to her. The strength of his grip on her right wrist told her she'd not escape this time until he was ready to let her.

Misty-eyed in anger and humiliation, she faced him.

"Please," Brian insisted, his high humor softened a bit by the fact that he was now short of breath from the immense effort he'd put into the pursuit. "Stay with me."

"Why? So you can make fun of me? I'm a quick learner, Mr. Forrester. I'm glad you had a good laugh, but now I have work to do. If you'll excuse me?"

His thumb was making gentle circles on the flesh of her wrist, and Molly wondered why the air in the mall seemed so rarified. After all, they were only on the third level. There couldn't be any significant change in atmospheric density due to elevation, could there?

Fremont obligingly stepped aside so Brian could reach Molly's other wrist. He pulled her closer and spoke softly, privately, while the rest of the world passed by in another realm.

"Don't you see what made me laugh?" he asked. "It wasn't you. It was what you did. Nobody's done anything so wonderful for me in too long to remember. My reaction was sheer, gut-level relief."

There was no guile in his eyes, only truth. Molly wanted desperately to lean closer, brush his mouth with a kiss and assure him he was the most appealing man to come into her life since . . .

She stood very still, shocked that she'd have such an intimate thought toward a man she didn't know. An even bigger shock was the fact that no other memories had surfaced to remotely challenge the unsettling feelings she was already having toward Brian Forrester. That realization scared her to death!

Her eyes widened. Just that morning, celebrating life in the warm sunshine, she'd known this day was going to be special. But not *this* special. This was . . . unbelievable.

Brian's grip began to relax. "I take it from the look on your face that you've decided to stay with me for a little while?"

"I have." Molly smiled and straightened, sorry to have to relinquish his touch.

"Good." Grinning widely, Brian looked up at her. "You can help me pick out a gift for Joyce."

Chapter Two

All the sunlight seemed to go out of the morning for Molly. "Terrific. Is Joyce your wife?"

"My brother's wife," Brian said, raising one eyebrow. "Now smile."

"I was."

"Until I mentioned Joyce, you were," he teased. "I'm beginning to actually believe you're interested in me."

This was going too far too fast. He needed to know she was not in the habit of letting men pick her up in shopping malls or, for that matter, anywhere else. Once again she blushed.

"Don't get smug, mister. I don't usually take up with strangers."

"Unless they have great muscles?"

Brian was not going to make this easy, she could tell. Still, he'd had enough problems lately. If one pleasant afternoon lifted his spirits, then Molly would not grudge him the time. She'd never see him again, of course. She had her career to concentrate on, to lend purpose to her existence. Romance of any kind with anyone was out of the question. Given the painful examples her parents and siblings had set, she'd decided long ago to cling to the sweet bliss of single life.

"I work out," Brian was saying. He stared up at her. "Hey. Molly Evans. Are you there?"

"I'm here. Shall we go?"

Fremont placed himself between her and Brian's chair and began keeping perfect pace as they started off. Molly smiled, pleased with the dog's natural instincts.

She lifted her gaze to rest on Brian's handsome face. "Let me tell you something about my job. I think you'll find it interesting."

He reached down to rest one hand briefly on the dog's strong spine, then went back to propelling his chair.

"I know I will," Brian said, nodding. "I already do."

For Brian, the time passed in a whirling blur. He and Molly had found perfect gifts for his family on the ground floor, then returned to the mall's third level to share lunch at the fast-food court. He knew he was grinning like an idiot, but he couldn't help himself. Since the accident, he'd been acutely aware that such special moments of life were too precious to let pass unappreciated.

"So what'll it be?" Brian asked. "Chinese, burgers, hot dogs, Italian?"

"I'll take care of my own," Molly said. "But thanks."

"Oh, no, you won't." Coasting ahead of her, he pivoted, blocking her path. "You helped me when I was in need, and now it's my turn."

She laughed softly. A lock of his hair had fallen across his forehead, giving him the most endearing appearance. How could she refuse? "Do I look like I'm in need?"

"Definitely," he countered. "It's plain you're about to faint from hunger."

"In that case, I'd better sit down," she said, plopping wearily into the nearest chair. "Whew! Between keeping up with you and training Fremont, I'm pooped."

"How about burgers with the works?" Brian asked.

Molly nodded. "And a Coke soft drink?"

"And fries."

"Whoa. I want to be able to fit into my van when this afternoon is over. Hold the fries."

"Right." Pivoting, Brian joined the nearest line. It was moving slowly, but all the better, he reasoned. He needed time to think.

Looking back, he saw Molly lift her arms over her head to stretch. The action pulled her T-shirt tightly across her chest, outlining the shapely breasts she was apparently trying to camouflage. He shook his head. Why was

Molly Evans so open about so many things, yet so reticent about others, particularly her personal life? He'd tried more than once to get her to talk about the man or men in her life, and she'd skillfully sidestepped his queries.

Brian shrugged. It didn't matter. At least not to him. He had no right to entertain ideas about any woman, let alone one as pretty and intelligent as Molly. He gripped the arms of his chair, his muscles flexing. Pamela had been right. Cruel, but right. When she'd kissed him off for good and opened his eyes to the reality of his situation, she'd done him a big favor.

Molly caught him looking at her, raised one hand and waved. Brian returned the friendly gesture. Anyone else would have insisted on helping him carry the food, but not Molly Evans. Beginning to smile again, be studied her face, his personal pride swelling. If Molly was afraid of his dropping her lunch on the floor, she didn't show it. The unspoken compliment touched him deeply.

Wheeling up to the counter, he ordered and paid, then moved to the pick-up area. The food came on a tray, giving him the option of balancing it on his lap and using both hands to maneuver the chair. When he reached the table, Molly waited for him to hand her the tray.

"Made it!" Brian said with a grateful sigh.

"I knew you would."

"You did, didn't you?"

"Of course." She helped herself to a hamburger. "Why would I doubt you?"

"Because I often do, myself," he said quietly. Ignoring his food, he reached for her hand, closing his fingers around hers. "Being here with you today is the most fun I've had in a long, long time. I want you to know that."

Molly's bite of hamburger stuck in her constricting throat and she had to fight to get it down. She couldn't admit, to him or to herself, how much his touch was affecting her.

"No sweat," she said. "It's all part of my job."

Her terse reply was too flippant to satisfy Brian. She had to know his confession was sincere, so why was she trying to make it seem as if her presence was of no consequence? Maybe he hadn't made himself clear enough.

"What I mean is, I'd like to see you again." From the way she stiffened and pulled away, he knew what her answer would be before she uttered a word. And why not? What did he think he had to offer a woman — any woman — let alone one as attractive as his companion? As impossible as it seemed, for a moment he'd forgotten he was stuck in that damned chair for the rest of his life.

Rather than wait to hear Molly's rebuff, he quickly gave both of them an out. "So when can I come to visit FFI?"

"Oh." Taking a deep breath, Molly forced herself to relax. Reaching into Fremont's backpack, she withdrew a brochure and handed it to Brian. "Here. This explains a little about our organization. Just call ahead for an appointment and we'll have someone show you around when you arrive."

"Thanks." He barely glanced at the glossy pamphlet. Nothing could give him back the life he'd lost, he decided easily. Being an auto builder and mechanic required mobility as well as strength, so that part of his life was over. What he really needed was two good legs again. Beyond that, there was nothing else.

"Read it," Molly urged. "I'll bet you'll be surprised."

"I'm sure I will be." Reaching down, he ruffled Fremont's velvety ears and the dog laid his soft muzzle across Brian's thigh. It wasn't fair to lead Molly on, pretending interest in the service-dog program at FFI just to be near her, but he couldn't let go of the feelings she'd awakened in him. Not yet. He had to see her again, if only to find out if the magic she'd already brought into his life could be continued, intensified. She'd made it clear by her actions that she wasn't interested in him in any but the most academic way, yet he felt driven to try to stay in contact with her. He shook his head. Apparently, desperation did funny things to a man's perspective.

Brian pretended to concentrate on his food while casting surreptitious glances at Molly. She was pretty, but not what professional photographers would call beautiful. Her hair was thick, shiny and neatly braided, not voluptuously cascading over her shoulders, and her clothing hid most of whatever feminine curves she possessed. So what was it about her that made his heart beat faster? What made his breathing grow labored when she spoke, fixed her sparkling hazel eyes on him, smiled or touched him?

In the final analysis, he guessed he'd have to call her special quality "love." Oh, not the personal kind, of course, but a love of life and living in general. She seemed to expect things to work out for the best. Consequently, for her, they did. And for all he knew, her optimism might be catching. He had to find out.

Brian slipped the brochure into an outside pocket on his chair. Molly Evans would be seeing him again soon, whether she liked it or not. He'd gotten a hazy glimpse of what it would be like to be accepted in everyday circles, and he was not about to let go of that vision until he knew how to make it happen when she *wasn't* around.

Jubilant, Molly burst through the office door, Fremont in tow. "Good afternoon, gang."

Three young women only a few years younger than Molly acknowledged her briefly before going back to work. The closest, a brunette whose desk backed up to Molly's, smiled and continued the conversation.

"Well, well," Bev said, raising an eyebrow, "what's come over you? Did you finally get Fremont straightened out?"

"I hope so," Molly said. "He's responding better every day."

"That's good." Bev handed Molly a stack of mail. "Why don't you take care of this while you're still in a good mood?"

"I won't be if I stop to do that now." Molly spun around to stare out the window at the parklike grounds. "Isn't it a beautiful day? Look at that sunshine. You'd hardly think it was February, would you?"

The younger girl paused to watch Molly. "You know, if I didn't know better, I'd swear you were in love."

Molly's head snapped around, her forehead

creased in a scowl. "Wash your mouth out."

"Well, I would. Of course, I've never seen you in love, so I have no way of telling *how* you'd act."

"No, and you never will, either," Molly vowed. "Love is for soap operas, fairy tales and suckers. If you don't believe me, ask my family."

Bev sobered. "Sorry I brought it up."

"Hey." Going over to her friend, Molly put one hand lightly on the girl's arm. "Don't take it so hard. I just have no use for cottages, picket fences and bluebirds. It's a personal choice."

"Or for princes?" Bev asked.

"Especially not for princes." Molly made a funny, sour face. "Too many of them are really frogs."

Bev giggled and seated herself at her desk. "I thought it was supposed to be the other way around."

"You tell it your way, and I'll tell it mine."

"Fair enough." A longhair cat had curled up under the drooping leaves of a houseplant that was balanced on the outer corner of the desk, and Bev had to push aside the cat's tail to get at her paperwork. "That's what I like about this place," she said. "It's never dull."

"Life is what we decide it is," Molly said,

starting toward the rear door to take Fremont to the kennels.

"Something wise your mother once told you?" Bev called after her.

Molly stuck her head back through the door and smiled. "Nope. She's never figured it out, poor thing, and I don't expect she ever will. I learned about life by watching what *not* to do to be happy."

Brian had picked up the telephone and begun to dial at least four other times before he finally decided to place the call. A young-sounding female voice on the FFI end of the line had made an appointment for him and promised a tour of the facilities.

Now, waiting in their enormous, sparsely furnished lobby, his mind whirling with ideas, he wondered seriously if he'd made a mistake. Even if he did manage to draw Molly Evans as a guide, there was the distinct possibility she'd be less than pleased he'd requested her. The girl on the phone had said she couldn't promise, but if he'd come, she'd see what she could do. Well, he'd arrived. Now it was out of his hands.

Speaking of hands, Brian noted, his were perspiring. He wiped them on his pants, straightened his polo shirt and took a deep breath. It wasn't that he was afraid. Many

33

times he'd faced danger or even imminent death on the race track or behind the wheel of an experimental vehicle without flinching.

He snorted derisively. It wasn't death he feared; it was life. And seeing Molly again. He hadn't figured out why, but she had become the most important element in his life. If she refused him the tour or passed him off to someone else, he knew the rejection would be damned hard to take.

A broad grin spread across his face as he saw Molly coming toward him. A small, furry, brown puppy with legs so short and stubby they were barely there followed closely at her heels. Brian held his breath, waiting, as Molly's face began to reflect the same enthusiasm he'd noticed before. Oh, dear God, she was actually starting to smile!

He gave his chair a push, coasted to a stop and held out his hand. "Hello, again."

The clasp of Brian's warm handshake shocked Molly's nerves with little prickly jolts that shot up her arm, traversed her skin, leaving goose bumps, then curled into a ball in the pit of her stomach. Telling herself to relax and smile, she realized she was already grinning so widely, her cheeks hurt.

"I told you I'd come."

"So you did."

"Where's Fremont?" He glanced at the floor. "And what's that?"

"This is Sam," Molly said. "He's a corgi."

Brian laughed and leaned down with his hand extended. The puppy licked it. "He doesn't look a bit like my brother."

"I beg your pardon?"

"Sam. Remember, I told you about Sam and Joyce?"

"Of course." She crouched beside the puppy, placing one hand on the arm of Brian's chair for balance. "*This* Sam is a signal dog. Or at least he will be. We will train him to assist the hearing impaired."

"Well he certainly has the ears for it," Brian remarked. "Looks a bit like a bat or a fox, doesn't he?"

Molly chuckled. "You're right. But don't tell poor Sam. He thinks he's gorgeous."

"He is cute," Brian said. "His fur feels like the down on a baby chick."

"I didn't know you were a farmer, too."

"There are lots of things you don't know about me, Ms. Evans. While I'm here, would you like me to remedy that?"

"I thought you'd come to learn about FFI." Cocking her head, she looked up at him.

"I did. It's just that our time at the mall was too brief to suit me. That's why I asked for you as my guide today."

Molly started to rise, but Brian was too quick for her. The hand she had rested on the arm of his chair was captured in his and held fast.

"I'd love to, but I really can't," she said. "I have too much work to do." Feeling his grip tighten, she knew she should resist him more strongly, yet relinquishing his touch was the last thing she truly wanted.

"And what I'm asking is selfish," Brian said. "I know that. But don't you see what you've already done for me?" He glanced around the spacious room. "I'd never have ventured out unassisted into strange territory like this even a few days ago, and now, here I am."

"I know you weren't scared to," Molly countered. "After all, I met you in a crowded mall."

He shook his head. "Not scared, Molly. Detached." Blinking, he looked hard into her eyes. "I didn't care, and now I do. The only thing different in my life has been meeting you."

With a sigh of resignation she stood. "Okay. I guess I can spare you an hour, but that's all."

"Done!" Brian's grin spread across his face.

Molly couldn't help returning his infectious smile. "Don't look so smug, Mr. Forrester. Our facilities aren't nearly as big as the headquarters site up north. A tour won't take very long." Scooping up little Sam, she opened the sliding screen door to the office where Bev sat, watching, and slipped the puppy through.

The younger woman winked. "Nice."

"All corgis are nice," Molly said, pretending to misunderstand the comment.

"If that's a corgi, I'm ready to be reincarnated as a dog," Bev whispered. "Did you get a load of those shoulders and arms?"

"Never noticed," Molly said smugly. "Take messages if anyone calls for me. I'll be giving a tour."

"Yes, ma'am. Are you planning on taking a long lunch?"

"No way. I'll be too far behind in my work for even a coffee break, thanks to our visitor. Besides, I brought my lunch."

"Okay. I just wondered, since your friend there was dropped off and his ride left."

"What?" Molly's head jerked around. Brian had silently rolled close enough to overhear, so she treated him as if he'd been a part of the conversation all along. "What's she talking about? Didn't you drive?"

He shrugged, looking about as innocent as the corgi who had by now taken the hapless cat's tail in its mouth and was tugging on it. "To tell the truth, I haven't tried driving since I got hurt. Didn't have anyplace I wanted to go till the other day."

Molly reached for a telephone and brought the instrument closer to him. "Okay. No problem. Call whoever brought you and arrange for a pickup in about an hour. That should give us plenty of time."

"Sorry." He raised his shoulders in a gesture of chagrin. "Can't do that. Sam's gone on to San Diego to get some engine parts, and Joyce works. Guess I forgot to mention that when we had lunch together."

Bev was silent, her eyes widening as her lips formed the words, *lunch together*.

"It was wonderful," Brian said in an aside to the curious girl. "From the time Ms. Evans made the pass at me in the elevator, I knew she was special."

Bev nearly choked. "Pass? Molly?"

"Oh, knock it off, Forrester," Molly ordered, "and come on. Since I'm obviously stuck with you, we might as well get started."

"That's just what I was thinking," he said, pivoting to run alongside her. "We're going to have a great morning."

She pushed open the outside door to the kennel yard and watched him go through. "I suppose you know quite well there are no taxis to be had in this rural neighborhood."

"I did live close by for most of my life, yes."

"That's what I thought," Molly said. "You're getting to be a real pill, you know that?"

"Uh-huh. And it feels great!"

Chapter Three

Molly glanced over the top of the open file baskets on her desk and through the screen to where Brian waited in the lobby for his ride home. She'd hated to leave him alone after the tour, but he'd insisted he didn't mind and she'd had so much work backed up on her desk, she'd finally agreed.

Amusing himself, he'd scooted out of his chair onto the rug and was playing tug-of-war with little Sam. Cute, she thought . . . *both* of them.

"What are you going to do for lunch?" Bev asked.

Molly checked her watch. It was already after twelve. She took a deep breath and pushed her chair away from the desk so she could stand. In the lower right-hand drawer of her desk was a paper sack containing a fairly modest lunch. She'd have to supplement it, of course, or they'd both starve.

Starting toward Brian, sack in hand, she paused. The sensible thing to do would be to offer to drive him home. On the other hand, he hadn't been any trouble. Having him around was actually quite pleasant.

Bev was waiting for an answer. "Well?"

"I'm going to feed him, of course," Molly said with a wry twist of her lips.

"That's what I figured."

"Oh, you did, did you? And what *else* did you figure out?"

"That he's a great-looking hunk," Bev observed. "If you decide you don't want him, toss him my way, will you?"

"There'll be no tossing around of hunks while I'm head trainer here," Molly told her. "You want reservations on Mr. Forrester, you see the boss lady. I think I saw her go into her private office with Keith and Jim."

Bev's short hair shook as she tossed her head. "That's okay. Never mind. Forget I mentioned it. I wouldn't dream of disturbing Ms. Claymore."

"I thought not." Smiling, Molly went to join Brian.

Sam noticed her approach immediately. Because Brian did not look in her direction, she could only assume he was purposely ignoring her presence. The corgi barked.

"Acknowledge me," Molly ordered. "He's telling you I'm here."

"Sorry." Pulling himself up into his chair, Brian bent to praise the little dog. "I guess I was keeping a low profile because I feel guilty

41

about being here for so much longer than your regular visitors."

"Oh, you mean the bunch of kids who came through here earlier? We run field trips all the time from area schools and service clubs. The tours vary."

"I honestly didn't mean to get myself stranded on your doorstep for the whole day. It was just that I figured there'd be so much to see, and Sam couldn't spare the time away from work."

Molly held out the paper sack. "I understand. You hungry?"

"Yes." He glanced toward the door. "But Sam promised he'd come get me on his way home. He should be here any time, unless he ran into fog closer to the coast."

"Oh." Molly was not surprised to find that she hoped Sam took his sweet time. "Well, you can sit with me and I'll share my lunch with you, anyway, if you'd like."

"I'd like. Very much. Do we bring Sam?"

"Not if you expect me to enjoy my lunch in peace. I don't seem to be able to turn off the trainer part of my brain. If there's a dog present, I always watch for opportunities to teach it."

"Makes sense." He accepted the sack she placed in his lap and watched as Molly escorted the corgi to the office and turned him over to Bev. By the time Molly returned, Brian was hefting the lightweight sack and frowning. "You were going to *share* this? There can't be enough food in here to keep one of us from emaciation."

"I don't eat much."

"Well, I do, and now that you've brought it to mind, I'm starved."

"There's a soft drink machine in the hall by the parking lot."

"*That's* real filling. How about a burger?"

"You like those, don't you?"

Brian shrugged. "They're okay. The best part is, the places you buy them aren't fancy, if you know what I mean." His glance darted to the wheels of his chair.

"That I do," Molly said. "You should see the dirty looks I sometimes get when I try to take a dog I'm training into a nice restaurant. You'd think I had a twelve-foot-long alligator on the end of my leash!"

Brian laughed, picturing Molly all dressed up and accompanied by an alligator waddling along wearing the bright orange-and-green FFI backpack. What would she look like in a skirt? he wondered. The word *sexy* popped into his head and he didn't argue with the idea. There was no doubt in his mind that Molly Evans would look like a dream in a dress. Feeling his cheeks getting warm, he decided to concentrate on the more ludicrous aspects of his fantasy.

"It wouldn't work," he said. " 'Gators are too short to jump up like your dogs do and turn on light switches. Besides, they'd scratch the walls."

She couldn't help but laugh, too. "You have a silly sense of humor, Mr. Forrester."

"Me? I'm not the one who takes 'gators to dinner."

"Neither am I." Leading the way, Molly started for the rear double doors that led outside.

"Then I guess it's safe to go with you," he said. "If you're sure there aren't any alligators."

"None the last time I looked." She eyed the small sack in his lap. "We will starve, though. I just remembered I was out of yogurt and fruit to go with my half sandwich, so I stuck in a couple of crackers instead."

"We could throw Fremont in your van and go cruising to one of those restaurants that gave you trouble. With me along, you're legitimate."

Molly shook her head. "No. Thanks for the offer, but that's not the way to win people over to our cause. Besides, I need a break, remember? Let's just be two regular people out for a burger and a good time, okay?"

"Regular people," he murmured. God, that sounded good. And with Molly, there was no chance of pretense. If she said it, she meant it. The more he was around her, the better he felt about himself. He wondered if she had any idea just how deeply she was touching his soul.

Molly laid her hand lightly on Brian's shoulder. "Hey. Are you all right? If I hurt your feelings about Fremont, I'm sorry. I know you only wanted to help."

"No, no." He looked up at her. Genuine concern filled her expression. If this woman didn't honestly know how much she was giving to him — how much she'd already given — then it was time somebody showed her. Placing his hand over hers, he grasped it and lifted her fingers to his lips.

The kiss wasn't meant to be theatrical or continental, it was simply a heartfelt gesture given in response to Molly's empathy. He did it because he wanted to. Because she deserved it.

Trembling, Molly stared. Plenty of boys and, later, men had kissed her, one way or another, but no one had *ever* offered her the tenderness Brian just had. Deep within, her soul cried out in sweet anguish, so frightened of the feelings he was kindling that it kept insisting she must turn and flee.

45

But Molly didn't. She smiled, her eyes misting with the same kind of tears she often shed when a particularly difficult client and dog finally struggled through to successful graduation and a lifelong partnership.

Brian saw a tear slide down her cheek. "I didn't mean to . . ."

Wiping away the moisture, Molly passed off her sentimentality. "Forget it. I'm a certified softie. Always have been. Sometimes it's an embarrassment, but it's not your fault." Reclaiming her hand, she gestured toward the door. "Shall we go?"

"You're not mad at me?"

"No, I'm not mad." How could she tell him she was an eternity away from anger? "But I am hungry."

"Okay. You drive, I'll pay."

"No way. This is my turf. Besides, you bought the last time."

"I know, but I thought . . ."

"Don't start thinking of this as a date, Forrester," Molly warned. "We're two friends out for a good time, and that's all. Got it?"

"Yeah, I got it," Brian said. "It just slipped my mind for a minute who and what I was."

"Oh, hold on." It was clear to Molly that Brian had misunderstood completely. She crouched beside him. "I have a rule," she said. "I never date within the organization, clients or co-workers. It's not businesslike."

"Sure."

Molly could see she was getting nowhere. Not only were Brian's feelings obviously hurt by her unfortunate choice of words, she knew that all the progress she'd seen him make was on the line. It didn't matter that she'd made the remark about not dating him in innocence. How he'd taken it was what counted.

She muttered a curse and started toward the desk where Bev was pretending to work in spite of the interesting conversation within easy hearing distance. Poor Bev was a hopeless busybody. At the moment, though, Molly was glad of it. She gestured for Brian to follow, waiting to speak until he pulled up next to her.

"Beverly," Molly said loudly, giving her friend a start, "how long have we known each other?"

She laid down her pencil. "About two years."

"And during that time, how often have you known me to date?"

"Anybody?"

"Anybody. How often?"

"Umm, you want the truth?"

"Yes." Molly waited. This was the second time since meeting Brian Forrester she'd had to swallow her pride, and it wasn't going down easily.

"Never, I guess," Bev said quietly.

"Thanks." Molly had been out with men a few times since Bev joined the FFI staff, but the experiences had been so lacking, she hadn't bothered to share them. Now she was glad. She tried to push Brian back to the exit, but he stopped her.

"Why?"

"Why what?"

"Why haven't you, you know . . . ?"

"I'm usually too busy for such nonsense," Molly said flatly. "My work is quite enough to keep me entertained." Besides, romance had a scary way of leading to something permanent, and she'd seen the hopelessness of that enough times in her youth.

"Why tell me?"

Why, indeed? Her voice softened. "So you'll know you still have a friend, if you want one."

"I want one." Brian reached for her hand. This time, though, she was quick enough to avoid him.

Her rubber-soled shoes made no sound on the smooth tile floor as Molly preceded him to the door. "Then let's go find some burgers before we both get more short-tempered from hunger than we already are."

"You're on," he said, rolling through the outer door while she held it for him and heading down the ramp toward the parking lot.

"Come on. I'll race you."

"That application letter is from Brian Forrester, isn't it?" Bev asked.

Molly blinked and nodded. "Yes."

"What do you suppose made him change his mind?"

"I don't know," Molly said. "The last time I saw him, he told me he was sure a service dog wouldn't help him live the life he wanted."

"Maybe he thought it over and decided it would."

"Maybe." Pensive, Molly held the letter to her chest and went to the window. How many times she'd thought of Brian Forrester since last seeing him. How many times she'd wished he'd come through the door, his handsome face brightened up with a smile, his deep blue eyes full of devilment, his quick wit ready to match hers once more in spite of the emotional pain she was sure he still battled.

She sighed. Knowing that her desire to see him might easily be her undoing, she'd prayed he'd disappear from her life. The apparently affirmative answer to those prayers had saddened her and made her miss him all the more, but as the days passed, she'd felt she was finally getting over the thrill of the memory of him. And now here was his letter asking for an FFI dog.

"I can't be objective about this one," Molly said. If she turned him down, she'd never be certain she hadn't done it because she feared involvement. If she approved his request, he'd come back to FFI and the warring within her heart would start all over again.

"Then give it to Claymore."

Turning, Molly smoothed the paper and glanced at Brian's words once more. Picturing him writing it, she felt a familiar knot form in her stomach. "I suppose I could."

"You should." Bev smiled at her. "And you know it."

"You're right." She started for her boss's office. Pausing at the door, she scanned Brian's plea once more, reluctant to let go of it. The words were his, all right. Molly could almost hear him speaking them. And his self-pity was apparently nearly gone. In its place, she sensed a growing sense of worth, of belief in himself. The realization gave her such joy, tears gathered in her eyes.

Sniffling, she knocked on Ms. Claymore's office door.

"Come in."

Molly wiped away the signs of her tears, smiled and opened the door.

Sarah Claymore was seated behind her massive desk. A small woman, she was nevertheless always obviously in command. Tipping her glasses forward onto the bridge of her nose and peering over the top of the frames, she acknowledged Molly's presence. "Yes?"

Molly extended Brian's letter. "This one is too personal for me. Sorry. I was hoping you'd handle it."

"Why? Is the person not qualified?"

"Oh, yes. He's even attached a letter from his doctor. He's a perfect candidate for a service dog."

"Then what's the problem?"

Molly felt her cheeks growing warm. "He's a friend of mine."

"Oh, I see." Ms. Claymore took the letter. "Very well. I'll read it and give you my decision."

"Thank you." Obviously dismissed as her superior went back to the paperwork on her desk, Molly left the office.

"Well, what did she say?" Bev asked.

"She'll decide."

"Did you tell her you have a thing for this guy?"

Molly bristled. "Don't be silly."

"Okay. Suit yourself."

"Well, I don't," Molly insisted. She busied herself with rearranging the papers on her desk without bothering to focus on them. "We're just friends. That's all."

"Have you seen him much since the day he took the tour?"

Turning away, Molly stared out the window. "No. Not at all." She glanced back at her friend. "Why do you suppose that is?"

"Well, you did go out of your way to make sure he knew you didn't think of him as a man you'd ever be involved with. What did you expect him to do?" Bev waited, hands cradling her chin, for Molly's response.

"The problem is, I *do* think of him as a man I'd get involved with — all the time." Molly's fingers closed into fists. "And I don't like it."

"Why in heaven's name not?" Bev asked, her voice rising.

"Because since he's a man and I'm a woman, there's no telling where it will all lead."

"That's the general idea."

Molly returned to her desk and sank heavily into the chair. "Not for me it isn't. My parents were two of the saddest individuals I've ever known, and both my sister and brother have followed in their unhappy footsteps. I refuse to fall into the same trap."

"Meaning?"

"Marriage, of course."

Bev's laugh was a strangled chortle. "Marriage? My God, Molly, you wouldn't even let him buy you two hamburgers in a row. What makes you think he had marriage on his mind?"

Chagrined, Molly leaned on her elbows, mirroring her friend. "He didn't have to," she said slowly. "*I* kept thinking of it, and that was enough." She straightened. "You don't understand. A long time ago I promised myself I'd never marry. It's like eating chocolates. If you don't keep candy in the house, you're not tempted. See?"

"And what will you do if Claymore approves him for a dog? How will you cope with two solid weeks of teaching that gorgeous hunk of candy?"

"Thirteen days . . . and I don't know," Molly said honestly. "That's why I had to pass off the decision. No matter what I did, I couldn't win." She jumped, startling the sleeping cat when her boss appeared at the door. Ms. Claymore was holding Brian's letter.

"Molly, I believe we've found the answer to a dilemma."

"Yes, ma'am?"

"Your pet project, Fremont, of course. This man sounds perfect for that headstrong Lab."

"But Fremont is ready, and Mr. Forrester hasn't completed any of his paperwork, yet."

"Push it through. Boot camp starts in two weeks, as you well know, and we can't afford to waste a good dog by washing it out if there's a chance of placing it."

"All right." Molly watched as Claymore tossed the letter into her file basket.

"Telephone him," the supervisor said. "The sooner he's prepared, the better."

Molly's hands were shaking, her mouth dry. When she closed her eyes, she could still see Brian's intense blue gaze, feel his warm lips grazing the backs of her fingers. Waking hours held instant replays of their time together; her dreams had provided even more. Now it was to begin all over again, and this time they'd be thrown together for almost a full two weeks.

The knot in her abdomen tightened, twisted, coiled. Brian. Fate had intervened and she was going to see Brian again. If she'd thought her fantasies were running wild before, what kind of shape would she be in at the end of boot camp?

She licked her lips, remembering how every moment with him had seemed special, important, extraordinary. Reaching for the telephone, she lay his letter beside it, found his number and began to dial.

Chapter Four

Grumbling to himself, Brian pulled the sleeveless remnant of a favorite sweatshirt over his
head and brushed the dust off his faded jeans.
He wished Sam had stalled Molly when she'd
telephoned instead of telling her how and
where to find him. His objection was not to
seeing her again, it was to her seeing *him* in
his own home.

There was still a lot left to do to properly
remodel the house he'd once considered perfect for his needs. Hell, he and Pam had even
started decorating the place in preparation for
their marriage. She'd probably be aghast if
she saw the different kinds of things he was
having done to it, now. Not that her opinion
mattered anymore. As far as Pam was concerned, the Brian Forrester she'd loved had
not only been injured, he had died in the crash.
It had taken him months to realize that what
had really died in those few excruciating seconds was his chance for happiness.

Disgusted at the morose turn his thoughts
had taken since Sam had relayed Molly's telephone message, Brian wheeled across the bare,

wooden floor of the broad, nearly empty living room and opened his front door to wait. At the end of the covered porch lay the stairs. Beyond those, a flagstone walkway bordered by brilliantly blooming ice plants led in a meandering arc to the drive.

He grimaced. The whole thing was pretty — and totally unusable. He'd need a ramp somewhere along the porch's edge, even if he kept the stairs, and a smooth, straight, cement path to the garage. As it was now, he couldn't even leave his own house to greet his guests without help.

Not that he'd had a surfeit of company, Brian realized, a little surprised that he hadn't paid much attention one way or the other up to that point. He made a guttural noise. Living with Sam and Joyce had cushioned him from a lot of truths, not the least of which was that most of his old friends had ceased stopping by to see how he was progressing.

Abstractly, he wondered if he'd have behaved any differently if the situation were reversed. In all honesty, he doubted it. How many professionals wanted to be reminded of the possible result of a moment's carelessness or of the harshness of fate? Hell, he was their worst nightmare in the flesh.

Brian rolled back, his expression grim. Them nothing. He was *his* own worst nightmare.

The approaching noise of a poorly tuned engine drew his attention. It was a wonder the vehicle was still running, it was hitting on so few cylinders.

His heart thudded against his rib cage, and he gripped the wheel rims of his chair. Molly's van had sounded like that when she'd taken him to lunch. At the time, he'd wanted desperately to offer to fix it for her, knowing that such an offer was ridiculous. Instead, he'd simply commented that she was in need of a tune-up and suggested Sam's services. Molly had thanked him and politely declined.

He saw her slow the old green van, check the number on his mailbox and turn into the driveway. The van rolled to a halt, coughed and popped for a few seconds, then was silent. In his mind, he saw himself walk out to greet her, take her hand and smile. The vision made reality that much more painful.

Molly peered out, spotted him in the doorway and waved. As she came closer, he noted that her jeans fit like a dream, that her sunny yellow shirt had delicate flowers embroidered around the neck and that she wore no jewelry. She didn't need its embellishment. All in all, she looked the way nature must have intended, purely unspoiled. In her hand, she carried a bulging manila envelope.

"Sam told me where to find you," she called,

making her way along the path.

"So he said." Brian coasted aside to let her enter. "If I'd been there, I would have suggested another place for a meeting."

"Oh." Molly had sensed his reluctance to have her in his home even before he spoke. It didn't surprise her. Since Brian no longer had control over many areas of his life, he was likely to be more sensitive about his private space. She clutched the envelope to her like a breastplate of armor. "I can come another time if you like."

He breathed deeply, noisily. "No. You're here. Stay." Eyeing the envelope, he ventured, "I take it this is about my letter to FFI."

"Yes." Looking around the high-ceilinged living room, Molly hesitated. "Is there somewhere we can sit and talk?"

"I sit *all* the time," Brian said dryly, "but I'm sure you've noticed that." Cocking his head to one side, he led the way. "Come on. Through here."

Nervously, Molly followed. There was an aura of intensity about Brian she hadn't consciously noticed before. Maybe it was because they were in his house, or perhaps it was because he was upset. Whatever the cause, he was radiating barely controlled power, and the surplus energy in the air made Molly's skin tingle.

"I shouldn't have barged in on you like this," she said. "I am sorry. It's just that a lot needs to be done in a hurry or you won't be ready in time for boot camp."

He locked his left wheel and pivoted. "I'm not joining the marines. I'm just getting a dog, right?"

"Right." Refusing to let his attitude dampen her enthusiasm, she smiled as she explained. "We call the owner/dog training program boot camp because it's so intensive. The next session begins in two weeks. Will you be able to attend?"

Shaking his head, he grinned ruefully. "Well, I did have a date to go water skiing and then had plans to drive at Le Mans, but I think I can arrange to cancel all that and attend your sessions."

Molly refused to be goaded. What she was doing was for Brian Forrester's own good. If he wanted to joke about it, that was his business, but as for her, she'd never been more serious in all her life. Opening the manila envelope, she spread its contents on the glass-topped dining room table and laid her purse beside it.

"Here's the profile we need completed first," she said, plucking the form from the jumble. "Then there are questions about the dog's care, feeding, safety and so on. The forms for your doctors to fill out will probably take the longest to get back, so I suggest you send them out this afternoon."

"Whoa. Wait a minute. When I visited FFI, you told me it sometimes took *years* to get a dog. I'm not ready yet, and neither is this house. What happened?"

"One hardheaded black Lab happened."

"Fremont?" He stared up at her. "You're offering me Fremont? Why?"

Molly blushed. "Because you're so strong, both physically and mentally. Fremont needs someone like you, and there's no one else on our waiting list who we feel can handle him properly. If you decline, he'll probably be washed out of the program."

"A dog can be washed out? I don't believe it."

Sighing, Molly sank into one of the wicker-and-metal chairs and leaned an elbow on the table. "Believe it. I've seen it happen."

"What a waste," he said, shaking his head. "All that time and training."

"Exactly." Bending closer, Molly searched his expression. There was the usual degree of vulnerability she would expect, having worked with lots of folks like Brian, yet beneath that she sensed the stubbornness and strength of purpose that made him the perfect choice to be Fremont's master. This was not a man who backed down, who shirked his duty, whatever came his way. It was probably that quality that had brought his recovery along so rapidly and would eventually override the psychological scars, as well. Brian Forrester would make it, Molly knew, even if he didn't realize it yet. And whatever he did with his new life, it would be enriched a thousand times over by the freedom working with Fremont would provide.

Suddenly her personal fears became inconsequential. Brian needed a canine companion in order to reach his full potential, and Fremont certainly needed Brian. Ashamed that she'd ever considered putting her own feelings above the concerns of her profession, Molly smiled at the handsome man who was scowling at her across the formidable stack of paperwork. Ms. Claymore had told her to push him through. At that moment, nothing would make her happier than to oblige.

Managing with difficulty to tear her gaze from his, Molly reached into her purse and withdrew two ballpoint pens. She tossed one to Brian. "Here, Forrester. Start by filling in the simple blanks — name, address and so on — while I sort out the others for you. We've got a lot of work to do before you're officially cleared to receive a dog."

Brian hesitated. Drumming the pen on the

table, he stared at her. "Maybe it's too soon. I thought I'd have more time to get settled here and finish the remodeling."

It was his sigh and the barely perceptible droop of his broad shoulders that drew Molly to his side. Crouching beside his chair, she laid her hands over his left forearm and felt the muscles tighten beneath her gentle touch.

"Better a little too soon than years from now," she said softly. "It takes two years to raise and train one of our dogs, and we rely heavily on donations, so we never know for sure about future funding. If you pass up this chance, I don't honestly know when we could offer you another dog."

He said nothing.

"The intervening months and years won't be wasted, Brian, but they won't be as full as they could be, either." She began to smile. "I know. I've seen the difference a companion or service dog makes." Unbidden, tears misted her vision.

Brian cupped her chin in his other hand and looked so deeply into her eyes that his gaze brushed her soul. "You care that much?"

"Yes."

"And you think I'm ready?"

The timbre of his voice prickled the hairs on the back of her neck sending an exquisite shiver down her spine. "You're ready."

Brian nodded. "All right. I'll give it a try." Pausing, he drew her nearer, his breath warm on her skin, his thumb caressing her cheek as he lifted her chin.

"Good." Part of Molly wanted to resist as he leaned closer. A stronger part of her refused to pull away.

"Are *you* ready?" he asked, his lips only inches from hers. Before she could answer, he lowered his mouth and kissed her.

How something so gentle and tender could short-circuit all her defenses, she didn't know. There was no demand in Brian's kiss, no hard plundering or sexual insistence, yet Molly was instantly on fire from the whispering brush of affection across her lips.

She knew she was trembling, but so was he. His muscles flexed. While one hand caressed her cheek so carefully, the other was holding on to the arm of the chair with a punishing grip. She had only to run her fingers over his forearm to feel the contrast.

Brian hadn't intended to kiss her, he insisted to himself. He'd just been so moved by her sincerity he couldn't help himself. And he was extremely glad he'd acted. He felt fresh, new, like winter had just ended and, with a bolt of lightning, spring had come.

Suddenly he was aware of another, altogether unexpected physical reaction. Thunderstruck, he froze, his attention diverted as surely as if he'd just been punched in the stomach. The sensations below his waist were minimal, but not entirely absent and he could swear . . . Oh, God. Was it possible?

Not daring to look for fear his astonishment would further his embarrassment, he released Molly and pushed away from her. He had to know, and he sure as hell wasn't going to investigate while in her presence. He wheeled around and headed for the kitchen.

"Okay," he called back. "If we're going to work here, I'm going to go make us some coffee."

Molly's reply of, "Fine," sounded a bit feeble and confused, but that couldn't be helped. He had to be alone for a second, not only to recover his self-control, but also to let his eyes confirm what he suspected.

Rolling to a stop beside the kitchen counter, Brian slowly lowered his gaze to his lap. A broad grin spread across his face. "Well, I'll be damned." It was true. Molly Evans had awakened more than his desire to once again become a useful part of society. For the first time since the accident and Pam's total rejection of what he'd become, he felt like a man.

Adjusting his clothing to ease the recent constriction, he thought about what his body's reaction meant. Doctors had assured him that there was no reason why he and Pam couldn't continue in a loving relationship, but he'd not been able to function. Consequently, he'd remained convinced that the diagnosis had been wrong.

"What was wrong, Forrester," he said to himself, "was the woman. You had the wrong woman all along."

Tears of relief sprang to his eyes. Thank God Molly wasn't standing there watching him act like a damn crybaby, he thought, wiping the sparse moisture away quickly. He couldn't remember having shed tears since he was a boy, and he wasn't about to now, but, damn it, it wasn't every day a man learned he was still a man.

Brian remained in the kitchen for longer than it took him to start the coffee brewing. Finally he gave up trying to completely subdue his jubilantly soaring emotions and rejoined Molly.

She saw him coming. Whatever his problem had been, he seemed to have overcome it. Too bad he couldn't also help her get over his kiss. The sweet taste of his lips lingered, and she wished he didn't look so darned endearing. The best thing to do was what Brian had done, she decided: go on with their business as if nothing unusual had happened. The idea was easier to conceive than to implement.

She smiled, trying to make the gesture seem everyday. "I figured you'd call me if you needed help," she said. "Did you make out okay?"

"Oh, yeah," he said, blushing. "I'm fine. Just fine."

She regarded him quizzically. "You're sure?"

"Sure."

Molly laid aside her pen. "Good, because we need to talk."

"Uh-oh." He lost control of his smile and it split his face.

"Stop grinning at me like that, Forrester. I'm trying to be serious."

"So am I."

"You're not making it," Molly told him.

"Not yet, I'm not," he countered. "Actually, I haven't made *it* for quite some time."

"Brian! Stop teasing." She hesitated. "If I thought you were serious, I'd —"

"You'd what?"

"I'd have to leave," Molly said, her voice tinged with regret. "I already told you, I never mix business with pleasure."

He rolled closer and reached for her hand, disappointed when she evaded him. The smile faded slightly. "In that case, forget the dog and let me take you to dinner tonight."

"Absolutely not!"

"Why not?" Nodding, Brian answered his own question. "Never mind. I know why not."

"No, you don't."

"Then enlighten me. I'm all ears."

She paced away from him, then turned, her hands on her hips. "Because I like you, darn it. I really like you. And I refuse to let myself get sucked into a whirlpool and drown when I can still safely wade to shore."

"How'd we get in the water?"

"It's an analogy."

"It's stupid. You like me?"

"I said I did."

"Good. I like you, too. Come here."

She took another backward step. "No way."

"Oh, yes. There's always a way," he insisted. "I'm certainly beginning to see that."

With two strokes of his powerful arms, he'd closed the distance between them and nearly pinned her in a corner.

Molly dodged past him, across the living room. "Stop this foolishness."

He came toward her again. "You didn't think it was silly a few minutes ago when you kissed me."

"*I* kissed *you? You* kissed *me.*"

"And you hated it, right?"

67

"I never said that." She was cautiously edging toward the door. Not that she was afraid Brian would harm her. On the contrary, she was deathly afraid he'd kiss her again and she'd wind up throwing herself at him. One kiss they could probably ignore during boot camp. More and their working relationship might never recover.

"Molly." He held out his hand. "Come here to me. Please?"

So strong was the flow of energy between them, she started to comply. Then at the last second, she bolted for the door.

Brian couldn't believe she'd leave. Not like that. Before he could make himself stop and consider the consequences, he'd followed her over the threshold with a hard bump and on out the front door, rolling as fast as his strong upper body could propel the chair. Even when he saw her run down the steps, his highly emotional state refused to be overridden by common sense.

With one last tremendous push, he soared off the edge of the porch. For a wild moment he thought he might actually land upright. He didn't.

Molly had intended only to put the barrier of the stairs between them while she talked some sense into him. She'd never dreamed he'd try to follow her, or she'd never have left the porch. Seeing him fall tore at her heart.

The pain of landing brought him to his senses and he was mortified. *Idiot! Stupid, macho idiot. You wanted to prove you're a man? Well, you proved exactly the opposite. I'll bet she's really attracted to you now!* Cursing under his breath, he took a mental inventory and decided he wasn't hurt. At least there was that much to be thankful for.

Molly knelt beside him. Thank heavens the grass had cushioned his fall. If he'd landed on the stone path, he could have been seriously injured. Reaching out, she smoothed the hair off his forehead. "Oh, Brian."

With a jerk of his head he escaped her touch. He couldn't bear her pity.

"Are you all right?"

"No. I'm paralyzed. Don't tell me you haven't noticed. Whole men seldom go careening off porches and land on their faces in the dirt."

"Brian, please." Molly reached to lift the chair off him.

He raised on his elbows. "Is my chair broken?"

"No." She righted it and held out her hand to him.

"Good. Then get out of here," he ordered, ignoring her offer of help.

"We need to get you back inside first,"

Molly said calmly.

"We? There is no *we*, Ms. Evans, and if I weren't such a jerk, I'd have realized it sooner."

"I didn't mean for you to get hurt," she insisted.

"Hurt? You mean this fall? Lady, you don't have any idea what hurts and what doesn't. Forget it, okay? Just leave me alone and I'll do the same for you."

Molly stood and headed for the house, retrieved her purse and returned. He still sat on the lawn, the chair beside him. "I left the application papers." At this point, there was nothing she could do to salve his injured pride. She only hoped it wouldn't prevent his taking the right step in regard to Fremont.

"Fine."

She felt so badly about his predicament, she had to try once more. "Won't you please let me . . . ?" The hard-as-steel glare in his eyes kept her from finishing the thought or reaching out to him as she so desperately wanted.

Turning away, she put her sunglasses on to hide the turbulent emotion she knew must show in her eyes. Dear God, she hated to leave him there like that, but if she insisted on helping him, it would only make everything worse. His pride had taken a much more telling jolt than his body had. Starting the van, she

70

backed out and slowly drove away.

Brian watched her go. What a fool he'd made of himself. Who did he think he was . . . ? He shook his head and ran his fingers through his hair. Molly had done him more of a favor than she knew. For a short time he'd begun to think like a whole man and she'd opened his eyes to the truth. Hell, what would he have done if she'd agreed to kiss him again? And again. He couldn't very well point out to her that although parts of his body appeared willing, other essential parts were not.

Brian cursed aloud. What in God's name had he been thinking? He'd acted like a teenage boy with overactive hormones and no moral scruples at all. The poor girl barely knew him and his fantasies had her already ensconced in his bedroom. He deserved to be dumped on his face in the dirt for entertaining thoughts like that.

But that's all they were, he argued, just dreams, dreams that could never come true. A woman had always deserved more from her man than he could provide, like a home and family and some semblance of a normal life. That he couldn't promise Molly or any other woman. Pam had understood and saved face by leaving.

Well, fine. He pulled himself closer to the

porch, dragging the chair behind. Let them all desert him. He wasn't going to crawl again, at least not figuratively. If Fremont could give him the mobility to better care for himself, by himself, then he'd go ahead and apply. Maybe then he'd be able to stop kidding himself about someday leading a normal life with the likes of Molly Evans by his side.

Molly parked her van out of sight around the corner, locked it and started back toward Brian's on foot. If he seemed injured or unable to get himself and the chair back into the house, she would make her presence known. Otherwise not.

By the time she'd secreted herself at the base of his driveway behind a pink-blooming oleander bush, he had himself and the chair nearly to the porch. It looked as if he'd thought through the problem and had worked out the logistics of it. She bit her lip, hurting for him every inch of the way. He pulled himself up the steps, then hoisted the chair, placed it on the porch and set the brake.

Molly's nails cut into her palms. Oh, Brian. Behind her sunglasses tears gathered, pooled, then trickled down. Lord, she hoped he'd be able to finish the task of regaining the house without her, because if she had to help him and he noticed that she'd been crying, it would make the whole situation unbearable.

Straining along with his efforts, Molly used body language to urge him on. "That's it," she whispered, peering through the leaves, "use the post."

Brian did. His strong hands closed around the wooden support, his muscles flexed and he slowly, laboriously, lifted his body off the floor. Looping one arm around the post, he reached out for the chair, swung sideways and landed where he was supposed to.

It was then that Molly realized she'd been holding her breath. She let it out with a whoosh. He was all right. Safe. She could leave now. Only she didn't want to. With all her heart she wished she could go back to the instant when he'd asked for another kiss and this time give it to him. It and many others.

But she couldn't. The chance for casual affection had passed. Oh, Molly knew it was for the best, but that didn't make it any easier to accept. She watched Brian roll through the front door and close it behind him. For her it was as if the sun had gone behind a cloud. Sadly, silently, she walked away.

Chapter Five

So nervous she couldn't sit still, Molly cast an apologetic glance at Bev and managed to smile. "Today's the day."

"No kidding? Gee, to look at you I'd never suspect."

"It shows, huh?"

"Like a flashing neon sign." Bev checked under her chair for Sam and the resident cat before rolling the chair away from the desk. "You want me to go wait in the parking lot like 007 and report when Brian arrives?"

"Of course not!" The funny face Molly made at her friend was reflected in the windowpane. She *did* look harried, she decided, in spite of her new, blue FFI T-shirt and neatly pressed jeans. That was not a particularly solid image for an instructor to have, especially on the opening day of boot camp.

"The Del Rio girl is here with her mother," Bev reported, checking off the list she held, "and so is poor Albert Brooks."

Molly nodded. "I hope he makes it this time. He's sure not one to give up, is he?"

"More power to him," Bev said. "Any idea

yet which dog will be best for him?"

"Unofficially, I think Gaylord will suit him perfectly."

"And Fremont? What if Brian is too embarrassed to show?"

"He'll come," Molly said, hoping with all her heart that she was right. "He's filled out all the papers, and Claymore's passed on him."

"Did *you* make the call of notification?" Bev asked.

Molly shook her head in the negative. "No. I was afraid he'd hang up on me, so I had Keith do it."

"I'll bet that thrilled old Brian."

Blushing, Molly scowled at her friend. "I told you, there's nothing at all between Brian Forrester and me."

"Sure, sure. And that's why he took a dive off the porch while he was chasing you."

"You *promised* you'd not breathe a word of that," Molly reminded her sternly. "The fall was an accident, and I see no reason to embarrass him further."

"You should have let him catch you," Bev suggested with a sly grin. "Now you'll never know what might have happened."

"I know," Molly said, coloring more. "At least I have a pretty good idea."

The younger woman stepped closer. "Can

he . . . you know?"

"Beverly!"

"Well, I just wondered. Don't have a fit about it." She paused, grinning widely. "I'll bet he can, and even if he can't, I'll bet he more than makes up for it in other ways."

Of that, Molly had no doubt. The funny part was, she'd never questioned Brian's ability to make wondrously passionate love. That was part of the problem.

Keith, a lanky, dark-haired youth of twenty, hurried into the crowded office. "You should see what just arrived! I gotta go get Jim. He'll have a cow."

Both Molly and Bev echoed, "What?"

"A replica of an Austin Healey, only this one's got hand controls. You won't believe it. It's awesome."

"Brian," Molly said.

Bev concurred. "His profile said he used to build classic replicas."

"Let's go see." Molly was already halfway out the door, dragging Bev by the hand.

"You mean you're through being subtle?"

"I have never been subtle," Molly countered. "Besides, if there's a crowd looking at the car, he won't notice me."

"Hah! And you wouldn't notice him, right? Give me a break."

"Well, maybe he won't notice."

"Sure." Bev had caught up with Molly's quick strides and was patting at her dark hair to make sure it lay neatly in place. "And what are you planning on doing when you have to stand up in front of the class and lecture and he's looking right at you all the time?"

"I'm a professional," Molly said. "I'll just do my job." She came to a halt, staring. "Oh, my goodness."

"Wow. Keith wasn't kidding."

"No, he wasn't." Molly approached the bright red sports car slowly. If it was a sample of the work Brian's firm had done, no wonder his cars were in demand.

The top was open, revealing a built-in roll bar she doubted was stock, and next to the driver's door was the opening to a recessed area with clamps to hold his folded wheelchair steady behind the seat. The effect should have been awkward, considering the usually sleek, classic lines of the roadster, but it wasn't. She'd never seen any vehicle so gracefully designed and executed.

Mouth agape, she approached, drawing her fingertips lightly along the fender. "Oh, my."

Brian heard her. "It's a present from Sam," he said. "I didn't know it, but he'd been working on it since shortly after my accident. When he thought I was ready to drive it, he gave it to me."

Molly let her eyes meet his. In his mesmerizing gaze she thought she glimpsed both pride and apology.

"Molly, I —"

She waved her hand. "No. Don't say a thing. This is a new day, a new boot camp and a new start for everybody. That's all you need to remember."

Brian nodded. Leaning on the car door, he transferred from behind the wheel into his chair. "I had Sam install a special safety-harness system on the passenger side for Fremont," he said, starting for the building. "If it's not right, we'll modify it until it is."

"Good." Molly walked beside him. "Does your car have a top?"

"Yes, why?"

"At high speeds a dog's eyes can be injured by flying bugs or dirt. That's why we warn you not to let his head hang out an open car window."

"Okay. I'll work something out. Where is he, anyway? I can't wait to get started."

Molly halted outside the large foyer where other clients had already gathered. "Officially," she said quietly, "no dog has been placed yet. For the first two days, everyone will work with every dog. That way we can see if your temperaments are compatible."

"But I'll get Fremont in the end, right?"

She raised her eyebrows as she shrugged her shoulders. "No one can promise that."

"*You* promised that," he reminded her. "That's why I'm here."

"I know, and chances are very good that everything will work out as we'd expected. What do you want me to do, lie to you and tell you, sure, Fremont is yours, when it might not be so?"

"Of course not."

She smiled. "Good. I knew you'd be sensible. Come on. Let's go in."

Brian lightly touched her hand. "Molly?"

"Yes . . . ?" She didn't move for fear he'd break the contact, but he did, anyway.

"I'm sorry about the other day."

"Forget it."

"I should have let you help me," he said.

"Nonsense. I'll bet you did just fine."

As he propelled himself toward the open door, Brian smiled back at her. "You know I did."

She followed. "Of course I do. I was certain you'd — "

"Uh-uh, Molly. No lies, remember?" His gaze locked on hers and held it. "Thanks for caring enough to stick around till I was back on solid footing, so to speak."

"I have no idea what you're talking about."

Brian laughed. "Then why are you blushing, Ms. Evans? I swear, the color of your cheeks is as pink as the flowers on that big oleander bush at the end of my driveway."

"Oh." Molly lowered her lashes. "You noticed."

"Not at first," he said softly. "If I'd been thinking more clearly, I would have known you'd come back. You couldn't just abandon me like that, could you?"

Molly managed an embarrassed smile. "No."

"Once I cooled off, I realized how unfair I'd been." He extended his right hand to her. "Truce?"

She took it briefly, the tingle lingering long after her skin stopped brushing his. "Truce. As long as you promise not to chase me off the end of any more porches."

Brian chuckled. "No problem. Sam's already fixed a ramp for me so I can get to the garage myself and drive my Austin."

Pausing, she cocked her head. "You're not living with Sam and Joyce anymore?"

"Nope." He beamed proudly, a twinkle in his eye. "I'm officially back in my bachelor quarters just waiting to share them with someone special."

She backed away, her palms toward him. "Whoa. Don't start that again."

"I meant *Fremont*," Brian explained with

a laugh. "What ever were you thinking, Ms. Evans? Shame on you!"

Molly turned crimson, the heat from her flaming cheeks causing her whole body to flush. Fremont. of course. What else could he have meant? She wished the floor had a handy-dandy trapdoor she could plummet through. Anything would be better than seeing the recognition for her faux pas in Brian's eyes. Without a doubt, he knew exactly what she'd been thinking and was thoroughly enjoying her discomfiture.

Given the charted events of the next two weeks, Molly had no doubt he'd find plenty of new chances to tease her, too. That was all right. Let him have fun wherever he could find it. She could handle Brian Forrester or any other man who threatened her peace of mind and well-structured plans for the future. No problem. All she had to do was convince him *and* herself she didn't care.

Once boot camp was over, she'd assign Keith or Jim to the follow-up and never see Brian again. In the meantime, her best offense was a good defense, as her father used to say. If he hadn't applied the principle to his rocky marriage, it would have been good advice.

Molly placed her hands on her hips. "Forrester, stop causing trouble and get in there and get a name tag on, will you? We're almost ready to begin."

He saluted. "Yes, ma'am. Your wish is my command."

Molly turned away so he couldn't see the blush returning to her already warm cheeks. If her wishes truly were his command, they'd both be in deep trouble. Ideas she had no business entertaining persisted in flitting in and out of her conscious mind, and the memory of the touch of his lips was never very far from the surface, either.

She saw him wheel into the crowd, shaking hands and smiling as he went, and someplace deep inside her, an ache began to take form and grow. Exhaling, she heard a sigh, barely aware the mournful sound came from her.

"I'm happy single. I like my life the way it is. I'm happy, damn it — happy," Molly muttered.

Bev had come up beside her. "What?"

"I said I'm happy." Molly was scowling, and her reply was far too loud and forceful to go unnoticed, even in the large, crowded room.

"Well, good," Bev said. "Now, if you'd just try to smile a bit, maybe the rest of us would be able to believe you."

The silly face Molly made was unmistakably intended to be a parody of good humor. Her lips were drawn back, her white teeth gritted. "Better?"

The younger girl laughed. "Oh, much."

This time, Molly really did chuckle. "Good. Then let's get going. You and Keith round up the troops. I'll take Jim and go get the dogs. The sooner we start, the sooner we'll be done. It's going to be a long thirteen days."

By lunchtime, Molly was as tired as if she'd already worked the whole day. A large golden retriever named Gawain was giving everyone fits with his insistence on playing instead of working, poor old Albert was wrestling with his third dog, Anita Del Rio's mother was trying to boss everyone around, and Brian Forrester was being the most helpful, attentive student she'd ever had.

Humph. Darn him. Why couldn't he be a trial, cause a little trouble? It wasn't bad enough that she already knew he was a sweet guy in spite of his occasional gruffness, she'd now started to think of him as a big teddy bear.

She ran her hand over her hair, smoothing back stray wisps, and straightened her T-shirt. Heaven help her. How was she going to get through the next twelve and a half days when she was already so attracted to the man, it made her hurt to think about him? Darned if she knew.

Volunteers, bless them, had prepared a hot lunch and spread it out buffet-style in the rear of the classroom. Excusing her class, Molly made sure all of them had a dog under control and settled down beside each of them before stopping to fill a plate for herself.

Albert had wound up with Fremont, for the time being, and she noticed that Brian had pulled up beside him. She seated herself close by to listen. For the next two weeks, every interaction had to be taken into account. There was no lax time, no response or word that didn't count, as long as she and her staff were present.

"I like this one," Albert was saying, nodding his graying head at Fremont.

"Yeah. So do I." Brian had opened his own can of soda before he noticed that Albert was still fumbling with the pop top on his. They'd each told of their various disabilities during the introductory session. Albert had muscular dystrophy. "You want me to get that for you?" Brian asked.

Albert handed it over. "Thanks. Some of the most simple things in the world are a real pain, aren't they?"

"You mean besides these dogs?" Brian handed the open can to the much smaller man with a smile.

"And women," Albert added with a conspiratorial wink.

Brian eyed his frail-looking companion. It was hard to believe the middle-aged little man had much of a social life. Still, he was probably looking at Albert's life with a jaundiced eye. After all, being confined to a wheelchair wasn't a new concept to everyone. There was probably a lot he could learn from Albert Brooks.

"I haven't figured out what to do about the ladies," Brian confided in a near whisper.

Albert laughed. "Neither have I, but that has nothing to do with the fact I'm in this chair. Women are weird."

"You can say that again."

"Have many of them tried to mother you yet?" Albert asked. "I hate that. It takes away your manhood, if you know what I mean. For instance, there's this neighbor of mine who drives me nuts. She means well, but with all her hovering and tsk-tsking, I swear, there are times I'd gladly give her a swift kick if my legs would cooperate."

Brian took a sip of soda, then set the can down. "Mostly it's me who needs a kick," he said. "I seem to get mad all the time. I never used to be like that."

"You're new at this, I gather."

"Fairly."

"Be patient. It'll come."

"I'm not sure I want to get used to it,"

Brian confessed. "I hate being like this."

Albert reached over and patted his arm. "You know that phrase they use for recruiting, 'Be all that you can be'?"

"I guess I've heard it."

"Well, apply it. None of us are ever exactly who or what we'd like to be, disabled or not. If you think about what you've lost, it'll make you crazy."

"It already has."

Grinning, Albert raised his thick, gray eyebrows, then winked at Brian. "I've got just the cure for you. There's this great square dancing club I belong to. We meet on Mondays. Molly said we're not taking the dogs home with us for a few more days, so I can still go. Why don't you come along tonight?"

Brian choked on a bite of food and coughed noisily. "Square dancing? You've got to be kidding."

"Not at all." Albert poked Brian in the ribs. "Lots of good-looking women like to dance. If we went in your car, we'd have to beat them off."

"But . . . us? Dance?"

"I've got a motor," Albert said, laying his hand on the controls on the arm of his chair. "You'll have to work harder, but I guarantee you'll have a ball."

"That's nuts," Brian argued.

Albert was nodding his head. "Okay. Have it your way. I'll think of you when Lillian is riding around on my lap." With that, he spoke to Fremont to get the dog to his feet, then wheeled back to the table for a second helping.

Pensive, Brian fell silent. Why couldn't he picture himself doing the kinds of things Albert had suggested? Was it so farfetched? He guessed not, yet every time he imagined himself in any situation, he was on foot, his old self, capable and in charge. The closest he'd come to recapturing those feelings in real life was when he was behind the wheel of the Austin.

He sensed someone's eyes on him. Looking over his shoulder, he saw that Molly was seated only a few feet away. Suddenly he wished he hadn't joined the other man in his good-natured critique of women.

Brian blushed slightly. "Hi."

"Hi."

"Been there long?"

"Uh-huh."

"Oops." He smiled. "Sorry."

Molly laughed lightly. "Relax, Forrester. I'm not the enemy, no matter how weird you think I am."

"We didn't mean you," he quickly insisted. "The reference to women was general. Besides, I'm glad you're here. I want to thank you."

"For what?"

"For not coddling me the way Albert described. I used to think it was worse being ignored because of this chair, but I've changed my mind. Being constantly fussed over has got to be awful."

"Well, don't worry," Molly said, getting to her feet to help clean up the table. "I won't treat you as if you're fragile, body or ego."

"Thanks . . . I think."

She laughed warmly. "You're welcome." Raising her hands over her head, she clapped them. "Okay, everybody. Listen up. It's time to switch dogs again. Albert, you give Fremont to Brian and take Gaylord. Anita, pass Noodles to your mother to hold, and Jim will fasten Susie to your chair. That's it."

A sense of peace and rightness came over Molly as she watched the five people change dogs. Brian and Fremont were happy to see each other, and Albert seemed to have Gaylord in hand. Anita's cerebral palsy made her motions jerky, but the female black Lab, Susie, was patient. Gawain, Jim gave to Mr. Watkins, the stroke victim who could still walk, although haltingly, and Puddin', a gentle, yellow Lab, went to Robin, the little girl whose rare disease, osteo genesis imperfecta, made her bones break so easily, she could receive a fracture by simply sneezing.

Molly smiled. This was how the dogs and prospective owners would probably be matched tomorrow and from then on. She glanced at Brian. His head was down and he was praising Fremont for little more than being there. The pair had bonded already, so much so that the dog was constantly checking to see if Brian wanted or needed anything. That was the way it was supposed to be. A chill shot up her spine, tickling her scalp.

Sighing, she turned to erase the chalkboard in preparation for the next lesson. Being near Brian Forrester was wreaking immense havoc on her nervous system, but it couldn't be helped. Everyone here, people and dogs, depended on her. She wouldn't let them down. Training FFI dogs was much more than a job to her; it was a duty to mankind, a sacred trust.

Licking her lips, she steeled herself, then turned back to face the class and began the afternoon lesson.

Chapter Six

Molly was amazed at how adept Brian had become by the end of the first week, not to mention the second. He'd mastered his own dog, then gone to work helping Albert control Gaylord, and it looked as if Albert was finally going to graduate.

She saw Brian practicing off to one side for the final exam with Fremont. They were a perfect pair, headstrong, muscular, intelligent and all male. A thrill shot through her, traversed her skin with a shiver, then settled in her innermost being. Brian always did that to her; looking at him, hearing his voice, simply knowing he was around.

Not that she couldn't control her urges a little longer, she argued. After today she'd be free of temptation. The solo for each pair was this morning at the Escondido Mall, where she and Brian had met, and she felt certain all her students would pass.

Brian looked up. Molly met his gaze, smiled and walked over to him. By now, Fremont knew better than to greet her without permission, so she ignored him in order to strengthen the training.

"Are we ready?" Brian asked.

Nodding, Molly said, "Beautifully. I'm impressed."

"I wouldn't have dreamed these dogs could do so much." His hand rested on Fremont's broad head.

"When you get him home for good, you'll realize how much more he can do. Don't be afraid to ask a lot of him. He'll be happiest when he's working."

"Just like you?" Brian observed.

"This job is my life." Molly's voice mellowed. "I know it sounds old-fashioned, but it's my calling."

"And for that, I know we're all grateful," Brian said. "But what about the personal side of Molly Evans? There must be more to life than working."

"Not for me, there isn't."

"There should be."

"Who says?" She could see that he was ill-at-ease speaking to her so bluntly, and she wondered why he'd chosen that particular time to express his beliefs.

"I say. So does Albert."

Molly humphed. "Oh, so that's it. Seems to me you need to take some of Albert's other advice and stop mothering me. I can take care of myself."

"Taking care of yourself is not the same as having someone special who cares about you, Molly. I know."

She struggled to keep her voice calm, her demeanor casual. This was exactly the kind of exchange she'd feared most. "And you're volunteering for the job? Well, thanks, but no thanks. I'm fine just like I am."

"Whoa. Wait a minute. I didn't mean that *I* wanted to be considered."

That stopped her cold. Of all the men she'd ever met, only one had the ability to make her tremble with a look or go weak-kneed in his presence, and there he sat, telling her he wasn't interested. Terrific. For the past thirteen days she'd agonized over her latent feelings and chastised herself repeatedly for coveting Brian Forrester — all for nothing.

She faced him, hands on hips. "Thanks a bunch."

"Don't go getting all huffy on me."

"And why not? What makes you think you have the right to give me personal advice? And who did you have in mind to rescue me from my awful life of solitude?"

"Hell, I don't know. What difference does it make?" Brian noticed that Fremont had gotten to his feet and was watching him.

"I figure the least you could do is find me a rich, good-looking man to start me off on the road to bliss," Molly said.

"Now you're being facetious."

"And you're being ridiculous. Why should I change a life that's already happy, huh? Why? If you think a single life is so bad, why aren't *you* married?" From the devastated look on his face, she knew instantly that she'd opened a barely healed wound in his heart. It was too late to take back the question, so she waited and said no more.

His jaw muscles clenched and a scowl creased his forehead. "I was engaged to be married once," Brian told her. He glanced at his legs. "But she couldn't adjust to *this*."

"I'm sorry."

Forcing a smile, he looked up at Molly. "I'm not. If she'd gone through with the wedding out of pity, she'd have ended up hating herself and me. It took a lot of courage for Pam to tell me the truth."

"I suppose she was afraid of the unknown," Molly ventured. "That's not unusual. Maybe later, you and she —"

"Oh, no. You don't get it, Ms. Evans. I'm a loathsome creature. She couldn't even bear to look at me, let alone touch me. It was as if she was afraid some of my disability would rub off on her." He laughed, the sound hollow and bitter. "She's long gone. The last I heard, she'd married some CEO from San Francisco and moved up there." He stared at Molly. "Why do you think it meant so much to me when you said you found me attractive?"

"I did. I do." She owed him that.

"Fine. Consider me convinced. The point is, if you can find *me* attractive, like this, there are bound to be lots of more capable guys in the world who'd be right for you."

But none that I'd consider, Molly thought. In or out of his chair, Brian was the only man who'd ever made her think seriously about love, romance and the events that usually followed. That's why she'd tried so hard to avoid him during boot camp.

She shook her head in the negative. "Why the concern?"

"Because I feel like we're friends," he said quietly. "And to me, you seem lonely."

"Takes one to know one?"

"After graduation tonight, I'll have Fremont." At the mention of his name, the big Lab laid his velvety muzzle across Brian's knee. "He'll keep me warm at night."

Molly had had enough of their serious conversation. The more Brian said, the more he tore at her heart's buffer zone and the closer he got to the part of her soul she shared with no one.

She raised one eyebrow and grinned at him. "Ah, but can he cook?"

"Probably," Brian said, returning her grin as he patted Fremont's head. "Every day he surprises me more. I can hardly wait to get him home and try to discover all the other things he can do." He sobered again, reached for Molly's hand and squeezed it briefly before releasing it. "The hard part will be saying goodbye to everyone here."

"It's always hard for me, too, but gratifying."

"Will you at least think about what I said?" he asked.

For Molly, there was little question about that. Every word Brian Forrester had ever said to her, every glance he'd shot right into her soul, every laugh they'd shared together — all were a permanent part of her and always would be. He'd already become a regular character in her dreams, waking or sleeping, and she couldn't imagine a day without him any more than she could picture spring without flowers and sunshine.

Of course, she couldn't tell him that. He'd made it perfectly clear that he wasn't interested in her any more than she'd permit herself a continuing interest in him. It was better that way. Once parted, they'd forget, or at least she believed he would. As for her, she knew she'd carry the images of Brian Forrester near to her heart for the rest of her days.

"Will you?" he pressed. "Promise?"

"Yes. I promise I'll think about what you said."

"You'll find somebody. I know you will."

"Sure," Molly said with a wan smile. "Like my mom and dad did." Brian looked so pleased with himself and so satisfied with her reply, she didn't have the heart to go on. It was enough to have watched the pain and destruction of her parents' marriage, then those of her siblings, without sharing the story.

She might be the youngest in her family, but she wasn't naive. There were only two elements in life that could be trusted: oneself and the love of a faithful friend in dog's clothing. The latter was one of the reasons she'd become a trainer.

Nodding farewell, Molly excused herself from Brian and began to check on the other students and dogs. All were doing well enough to graduate, even Albert. Pride swelled within her. There was plenty of reward in her job to satisfy all her needs, she affirmed. Never once had she regretted leaving her position as a physical therapist to come to work for FFI.

So why was her heart divided and warring within her? she wondered. And why did she get all choked up every time she thought about never seeing Brian again? The answer was so obvious, Molly couldn't deny it. She cared about and for him. Not that it mattered. It was simply a fact, painful but true.

He must never guess, of course. That would be cruel, because nothing could ever come of her feelings, no matter how strong they were. Brian needed exactly what he had prescribed for her — a mate. And she would never marry. Only fools and romantics did that. Molly Evans was neither. She was a realist.

Molly wore her favorite white dress to graduation. It had short, lacy sleeves, a gathered waist and a fitted bodice. She liked the simple elegance. Moreover, it was the only really good dress she owned and was new to each succeeding batch of graduates, so it was perfect.

The ceremony promised to be touching. Rehearsal had gone well, and dinner was over. Brian, looking more handsome than ever in a sport coat and slacks, introduced Molly to Sam and Joyce before everyone returned to the high school gym to join friends and relatives at the graduation and the party to follow.

Molly extended her hand. She would have known Sam without Brian's introduction. He had the Forrester blue eyes and muscular build, but she couldn't help noticing that of the two, only Brian made her heart beat faster.

Sam smiled, pumping her hand as if she were a long lost friend. "Glad to meet you," he said. "Really glad." He stepped aside and drew a slender blond woman forward. "And this is my wife, Joyce."

"My pleasure," Molly said. The older woman's handshake was firm, a surprise to Molly since Joyce seemed shy.

Joyce smiled. "The pleasure is all of ours. You've done so much for Brian."

"FFI does a lot for many people," Molly countered, slightly embarrassed to find so much attention focused on her instead of the service-dog project. "It's about time for the big moment. Shall we go?"

As the others followed her lead, Molly found she felt a touch more pride than usual. It was good to hear confirmation that your life was worthwhile, especially when parts of it wouldn't bear your own close scrutiny.

The gym was decorated with red, white and blue streamers, its interior filled with both chairs and wheelchairs. Puppy raisers had come to watch the fruition of their work, and Molly said a silent prayer of thanks for their selfless dedication. Without them, there would be no dogs to graduate.

Amid laughter, tears and well-deserved applause, FFI dogs and students paraded across the stage to receive their diplomas and offer short acceptance speeches. As usual, Molly found tears of happiness springing to her eyes. Brian's speech was the shortest. He merely said, "Thank you."

The crowd began to mill around as soon as the last diploma was awarded. Jim, Keith and some guests got rid of the folding chairs so there would be more room for maneuvering. It was Albert Brooks who first approached Molly. By his side was a strikingly pretty, petite woman in a brightly flowered dress.

"I'd like you to meet my Lillian," Albert said. "Lillian, this is Molly. Molly, Lillian."

The two women shook hands. Molly smiled. "Pleased to meet you."

"The same to you," Lillian said, her hand resting protectively on Albert's shoulder. "I understood you worked miracles, and now that I see it, I believe it."

Molly blushed. "The dogs are very bright. We breed and raise them ourselves, up in Santa Rosa."

"Why such unusual names?"

"We run out," Molly said. "And if there's a litter of nine or ten, it's really hard. You see, each litter is assigned a letter of the alphabet — *A, B, C* and so on. Gaylord came from a *G* litter. Makes it much easier to trace and compare results that way."

"Oh, I see," Albert said. "I'd wondered about that, myself." He patted Lillian's hand. "You were so smart to ask, my dear."

"And pretty," Molly told him, much to his obvious pleasure. "No wonder you talk about her all the time."

"I do, don't I?" Albert grinned. "She's agreed to be my wife."

"Oh, Albert, Lillian, congratulations," Molly said, tears coming back to her eyes in an instant. "I'm so happy for you."

She sensed Brian was close by and turned to look for him, her smile radiant, only to find he was nearly at her heels. "There you are. Albert and Lillian are getting married!"

Brian rolled past to shake the smaller man's hand. "Congratulations."

"Thanks. I'm a lucky man."

"I agree." Brian backed off, Fremont at his side. "Well, keep in touch, okay? My brother and his wife had to leave early, and I've got to be going, too."

"So soon?" Molly asked before she thought.

"Why not?"

He seemed to be waiting for her to say more — to say too much — and she wasn't going to fall into that trap. "We always celebrate a little after graduation. There's a cake and everything. I just thought you'd enjoy the party."

"I'm not much for parties," Brian said. He shook hands with Lillian. "Nice to have met you. I'm sure you two will be very happy."

Albert and his future bride both thanked him. As Brian wheeled away, Molly followed, her eyes downcast. It wasn't until they'd reached his car in the parking lot that she spoke. "I hope so."

"You hope what?" Opening the passenger door of the Austin, Brian ordered Fremont in and fastened the seat belt around him.

"That they'll be happy."

"Why wouldn't they be?"

"A better question is, why *should* they be?"

He faced her. It was growing dark, but he could still see her expression. It was unreadable. "You mean because Albert's in a wheelchair."

"No. It's not that. It's the idea of marriage," Molly said. "I've never seen it work, at least not well."

"You're kidding."

"No." She shrugged, folded her arms against the chill of her thoughts and the foggy evening air, and rubbed her upper arms. "In my experience, people are always better off single."

"What experience?" Brian asked. "Were you married?"

Molly's giggle was a nervous titter. "Perish the thought."

"Then you can't know."

"Oh, yes, I can. I don't have to be hit by a speeding bus to know how painful it would be."

Silent, Brian watched her, trying to see through to her real feelings. It almost seemed as if she were explaining in order to convince herself over again of something she'd long ago decided.

"So you'll never marry?" he asked.

"Never."

"You have no designs on anyone and never will?"

"That's right." Something in the tone of his voice made her look to him for explanation. Deep within his gaze there smoldered a barely camouflaged desire that took her by surprise. This was the Brian Forrester she'd been attracted to in the first place — and more. This was the dangerous, exciting man she'd glimpsed a few times when his guard was down. This was the man who had kissed her, then chased her off the porch. If she turned and walked away now, she'd escape further confrontation. She didn't.

"Then come and say goodbye to me," Brian urged. He held out his hand. Already he could feel his body responding in anticipation of

Molly's nearness.

His breathing grew more shallow; his heart raced. Oh, God, how he'd wanted to touch her, to kiss her, if only for the sweet memory to cherish when she was gone. Yet he'd held off, not wanting to encourage her to care for him. Molly deserved better — much better. But now, as long as she was sure she'd never be serious about a man, *any* man, he could safely act. Thank God she'd told him before it was too late.

She took his hand, letting him draw her closer. When he opened his arms to her and pulled her down, she carefully settled on his lap, her free arm around his shoulders. When his arms closed around her, she held to him as if her life depended on it and felt her eyes filling with tears.

Don't cry, damn it, she ordered. *Don't you dare cry.*

"Look at me, Molly." Loosening his grip, Brian tilted her chin just as he'd done once before. There was a misty look in her eyes, he noted, as her lips had begun to part. No man could have resisted her at that point if he'd tried, and Brian had no intention of trying.

He cocked his head and brushed her lips with a kiss. The jolt to his system seemed like it shot clear to the toes he knew he couldn't actually feel. This was wrong, he kept telling himself, wrong and stupid and . . . the best thing that had happened to him since the accident.

Closing his eyes, he deepened the kiss, felt Molly's overpowering response and crushed her to him, blotting out the harsh realities of their real world.

Molly clung to him. She'd known being in his arms would feel something like this, only she'd seriously underestimated Brian's powerful allure. His aura touched and caressed every part of her; his hands left searing paths across her skin. Her core throbbed with a desperate longing that urged her to call his name, to offer herself as a sacrifice on the altar of sensuality. But that wasn't all, nor was it the worst of it. Being in Brian's embrace had brought her lying denial of her feelings into the open. She cared for him. Deeply. Irrevocably. And when he was gone from her, she'd be left knowing *exactly* what she was missing.

She tried to pull away. He drew her back. The pounding of her pulse in her ears was deafening. Molly laid a hand on his chest and took the measure of his heart. It, too, thundered. Her fingers crept under his open collar. Everywhere she touched him his muscles knotted and trembled.

Mimicking her actions, Brian caressed her

neck, then let his hand slide down to brush across her breast. She heard him gasp, then groan as he buried his face in the silky skin of her shoulder. His actions were gentle in spite of his evident desire. He was hard beneath her, his arousal just one more proof that he found her as irresistible as she found him.

"This is crazy," Molly whispered, her protest becoming a purr as he began kissing her throat and neck. "We shouldn't . . ."

"I know that, and so do you," he said. "But we've both wanted to do it for a long time."

"No."

"Liar." His voice was hoarse and vibrant with suppressed emotions.

"Yes," Molly whispered. "How did you know?"

Brian tasted her earlobe. "How could I not know?" She wriggled on his lap, and he held her still to stop her. "Don't."

"Brian, I . . ." There were no words that would change their situation, nor was it wise to prolong their parting.

"Don't be sorry," he said, loosening his grip and cupping her cheeks in his hands so he could look at her one last time. "Don't ever be sorry. I'm just glad you told me there can never be anything permanent between us, because otherwise I never would have kissed you again, and I'd probably have kicked myself about missing out on the chance for the rest of my life."

I won't cry, Molly told herself. *I won't.* She looked at his handsome, loving face, storing up an eternity worth of memories.

He kissed her again, the caress of his mouth more gentle. "You brought me alive again, Molly," he said. "For that, I can never thank you enough." In the background, Fremont woofed pleadingly.

"And I helped give you the means to live a more productive life," she added. "Take good care of Fremont."

"I will." Still breathing raggedly, Brian grasped her upper arms, lifted and set her on her feet before him. "You take care, too, you hear?"

"I promise." Lord, they were conversing as if nothing special had just happened between them! Molly's skin still burned, her heart was pounding, the feel of his lips pressed to hers had permanently branded them, and her body throbbed with a longing she wouldn't have believed possible. Yet there she stood, exchanging pleasantries and making small talk!

Brian managed a half smile. "Go back inside, Molly. The others will miss you."

Smoothing her hair, she glanced toward the gym. Bright lights shone from the open door,

106

music was playing inside, and the festivities sounded as if they were in full swing. "I'll bet I look a mess." The dampness in the air heralded another foggy night, and that kind of weather always made wisps of her fine hair curl wildly.

"You look . . . lovely," Brian told her. "Go. I don't want you to watch me get into the car."

"Why not?" She'd certainly seen him do it often enough already.

"Because right now, I feel like my old self, and I don't want to spoil the fantasy by having you see me as a . . . you know."

She bent closer, laid her hands on his shoulders and placed a kiss on his cheek. "All right. Goodbye, then."

"Bye." Brian waited till she turned and started to walk slowly away before he circled the car and got in.

Personally, he'd never particularly liked solitude, although he did understand how a person's past could strongly influence his or her choices for the future. In Molly's case, that was just as well, because he certainly couldn't be the man she needed, assuming she someday changed her mind about settling down.

Out of habit, he reached over, checked Fremont's belt and slipped a pair of safety goggles over the dog's eyes before starting the car. Then he gunned the engine and sped away.

With a lump in her throat the size of a full-grown Saint Bernard, Molly paused to watch him go. For weeks she'd been preparing herself for this moment, this parting, yet still it stunned her. All her talk about loving her singleness seemed contradicted by the immense void she felt now that Brian was gone. She should never have allowed him to kiss her, to touch her, to show her any affection, but it was too late to go back. Molly knew, without a doubt, that for the first time in her life, she was about to experience the true meaning of being alone.

Chapter Seven

The following Wednesday, Keith caught up with Molly as she checked on the new batch of eighteen-month-old dogs in the FFI kennel. The din from their barking was so loud, he had to shout to be heard.

"We got problems!"

"What?" She cupped one hand to her ear.

"I said, we've got problems!"

"Oh." Motioning him to follow, she led the way to the courtyard. The dogs continued to bark, but there, at least, it was possible to speak normally and still be understood. She turned to her younger helper. At twenty, he was only five years her junior, yet there were times, like now, when she felt more like his mother than his contemporary. It was obvious something had upset him a lot.

Molly put up her hand as a calming gesture. "All right, Keith. Settle down and tell me. Nothing can be as bad as the look on your face indicates."

"Oh, no?"

"No. Now take a deep breath and fill me in."

"It's the *F* litter again," he said.

Molly felt her heart jump. "We got Flossie and Frank squared away months ago. They were doing fine."

"You know I mean Fremont. We should have washed him out early, when the others had problems."

"That's nonsense. He's headstrong, sure, but when he left here, he was behaving perfectly." By now her heart had accelerated to the point to which she was sure its wild beating must be visibly shaking her sternum.

"Well, he's not anymore." Keith paced away from her, shaking his head. "When I visited Forrester, the dog was refusing to answer any commands."

"That's impossible."

"That was what I thought till I saw it."

"And?"

"And it looks to me as if the dog is on strike."

"No way." Never had a dog she trained to completion of the course failed to perform well. It just didn't happen. A dog's brain wasn't like a sponge, soaking up knowledge that could later be squeezed out. Once a task was learned well, all the dog's owner had to do was reinforce the training from time to time and the animal would willingly carry out his duties for the rest of his life. It wasn't complicated.

Molly scowled at Keith. "Is Forrester following the proper form?"

"He was. By the time I left, he looked pretty disgusted, though."

"No doubt. Do you think we need to bring the dog in for a refresher?" Molly held her breath, not sure whether she hoped the answer was yes or no.

"Nope." Keith pointed to the office. "That's why I came out here to get you. Forrester's on the phone. He says he'll forfeit the token hundred and twenty-five dollars he paid. All he wants is for us to take Fremont back."

"For good?" Molly's glance darted to the office, and she started off at a trot. "Why didn't you say so? The last thing an angry man needs is to be kept waiting on the telephone."

"I had to fill you in first, didn't I?" Keith's longer legs let him keep up easily. Following Molly into the office, he perched on the edge of Bev's desk to listen.

Molly pointed to the telephone and raised her eyebrows to Bev.

"Line two," Bev said. "He sounds pretty steamed."

Seating herself, Molly took a deep breath, lifted the receiver and pushed the flashing button. "Mr. Forrester? This is Molly Evans."

"I never should have let you talk me into this," Brian said. "I'm taking care of the dog instead of the other way around."

"He will need care," she countered. "You knew that when you got him." She was trying hard to keep her voice level, her anxiousness under control, so Brian wouldn't sense that she was so upset, she was trembling. It had always been terribly hard for her to deal with irate people. Years had passed before she'd realized her irrational fears went back to her childhood when she'd often accepted her father's alcohol-induced ire instead of allowing it to he directed toward her mother.

"The dog is a couch potato," Brian grumbled. "All he does is mope around the house. Hell, he won't even open the door to let himself out when he has to go."

"You're sure he can?" Molly couldn't make out all the words in the string of expletives Brian unleashed, but she heard enough to get the general idea. The man was livid.

"Can? He did it for a week and a half, every night when I brought him home from boot camp. Hell, yes, he can do it."

"Okay, okay. Calm down. I'll send Keith back to see what he can do."

"No."

"I beg your pardon?"

"I said *no*."

Molly cleared her throat, her fingers gripping the receiver so tightly that they were white. "Mr. Forrester, please be logical. No dog I have ever trained has acted the way you claim Fremont is. If you knew dog behavior, you'd realize you're misreading him. What you claim is impossible. He might get sloppy about how he responds, but he's been too well-conditioned to simply refuse everything you ask."

"I'll prove it to you."

"Keith will —"

"No. Not Keith. You."

"I'm sorry. I have a full schedule today . . . all week as a matter of fact."

"Then take the dog back. I like the big, dumb son-of-a-gun, but I don't need a pet in my life right now."

"Fremont's not dumb!" Molly was losing her temper. The man might as well be attacking the intelligence of one of her children. In a way he was, since the FFI dogs had long ago taken the place of family for Molly.

"He's the laziest, dumbest cuss I've ever had the misfortune to know," Brian insisted. "And if you weren't chicken, you'd come and see for yourself."

"Chicken? About what, may I ask?"

"About being around me, I suppose," he said. "Do you figure you're so weak, you can't

113

survive a second visit to my lair?"

"Don't be silly."

"Then come. If you disagree and can show me how to overcome Fremont's sulky temper tantrums, I'll reconsider keeping him. Otherwise, you'll find him on your doorstep tomorrow morning."

"I should just let you bring him back, then," Molly said, her anger making her more outspoken than she'd intended. "If you're that sure he's useless."

"And then what?"

He had her there. If Fremont couldn't make the grade with Brian Forrester, there was nothing to do but return him to the volunteers who had raised him. They'd started two more pups by now. Chances were they wouldn't have room for him, either. It looked as though Fremont was in serious trouble. She had no choice but to do as Brian asked.

She sighed. "All right. I can't get there till after six this evening. Will that be okay?"

"Fine. I'll be waiting."

Molly winced. His tone was still formal, but his choice of words made her nervous. "I'm coming strictly to work with Fremont," she warned. "Is that understood?"

"Perfectly."

"All right, then. Goodbye." Molly hung up the phone before she could change her mind.

Both Bev and Keith were staring at her.

"You're going?" Bev asked. "After what happened at graduation?"

Keith's glance darted to Bev, then back to Molly. "What happened at graduation?"

"Nothing," Molly insisted. "Absolutely nothing." She waved her hand in the air and left the room, muttering, "Absolutely nothing. No way. Uh-uh. Oooh, no."

"Is she nuts?" Keith asked.

Beverly only smiled. "I don't think so. If you know what's good for you, though, I wouldn't ask her about grad night again."

Brian hung up the phone and stared at Fremont, curled up at his feet. Damn, lovable, good-for-nothing mutt. He spoke his name, and Fremont got slowly to his feet, stretched and laid his soft muzzle in Brian's lap.

"You're a mess, old boy," Brian said, "but then, so am I."

Fremont wagged his tail.

"I don't suppose you'd like to help me clean this place up, would you?" He ruffled the dog's ears. "No, I didn't think you would.

With a big yawn, the Labrador sat down, looking up at Brian.

"Yeah, I know what you mean," he said, smiling. "I haven't felt all that energetic lately, either. I guess we do have a lot in common."

Pushing one wheel forward, the other back, Brian pivoted and started off toward the kitchen. Fremont followed.

"We're having company," Brian said, continuing to talk to the dog as if he had his complete understanding. "One of our old friends is coming by after work."

Opening the door to the dishwasher, he began to stack dirty glasses on the top rack. At his shoulder, Fremont checked the smell of each one in turn as Brian placed them.

"You'll remember her, I'm sure," he said. "She's real pretty and stubborn, just like you. She's also mad at both of us at the moment." He closed the top shelf and started on the lower one. "I figure by the time she's through with you, you'll wish you were back at FFI. Poor guy."

Still watching Brian's activities, Fremont responded to his kindly tone of voice by licking his face.

"Stop that," Brian sputtered, fending off the affectionate dog. "Didn't Molly teach you any manners?"

Fremont stopped, cocked his head and listened.

"That's what I said, you big lug. Molly. Molly's coming."

Beginning to pant, Fremont wagged his busy tail and woofed.

116

"Yeah," Brian said cynically, "she does that to me, too."

Molly arrived just before the pizza delivery truck. Since she was still outside, she paid the driver, accepted the pizza and carried it toward the house. It smelled heavenly.

"I hope you don't mind," Brian called from the porch. "It's a peace offering. I figured you'd be hungry. I'll reimburse you."

She smiled and joined him. "We almost had two of these. I was going to stop on my way over, but I didn't know what kinds of toppings you liked."

Dancing in circles, Fremont greeted her at the door. She looked from him to Brian. "This is the lethargic dog?"

"He responds to pepperoni," Brian said, wheeling away. "And so do I. Put it over on the table by the plates and I'll go get us some Coke."

Molly hadn't forgotten why she was there. "Let Fremont get them."

"Sure. You want your soft drink tonight?"

Scowling, she stared at Brian, her glance an order.

"Okay, okay. Fremont, come." As he wheeled up to the refrigerator, he noticed that Fremont had at least deigned to accompany him. "Get it," he said, pointing to the towel

117

tied to the refrigerator door handle.

Fremont nosed it.

"Get it. Pull! Come on, boy."

Sitting beside Brian's chair, Fremont yawned.

Brian tried twice more without success before looking back at Molly. "You see?"

Her mouth had dropped open. Everything Brian had done was correct. The dog should have obeyed. She nodded. "Try something else."

Pointing to the light switch on the wall, Brian said, "Up. Switch." Fremont didn't budge.

"I spent weeks perfecting that," Molly said quietly. "I don't believe it."

Brian rolled over to a drawer and got a knife for the pizza. "Neither did I. It's damned depressing."

"I agree." She opened the pizza box, set her purse beside it on the table, took the knife from him and began to serve. "What did you do to cause him to give up?" she asked, handing a filled plate to Brian.

He slammed the plate down on the place mat in front of him. "Me? Now wait a minute, Ms. Evans. How did I get the blame all of a sudden?"

"It must have been something you did. My dogs don't just quit like that." She served herself and, lacking a napkin, licked her fingers.

"Well this one did."

"That's impossible."

Going back for two cans of soda, Brian returned and handed one to Molly after opening it. "So you say. All I know is, I'm still trying to get settled here and he's more trouble than he's worth."

That could be said for his owner, too, Molly thought. It had taken every ounce of courage she could muster to visit Brian's house again. She'd imagined that his greeting would be passionate with sensual overtones and that he would want to sit her on his lap once more and kiss her till she was giddy. Instead she got pepperoni and an argument. Whoopie.

"I warned you at the start that Fremont was stubborn," she said.

"Sure, but he worked in class and later, when I first brought him home." He took another bite of his pizza.

"When did he stop obeying?"

"Right after graduation."

"And you had nothing to do with it."

"That's right."

Chewing thoughtfully, Molly popped a loose piece of mushroom into her mouth and licked her fingers again. There had to be more to the story that Brian wasn't telling.

He settled back, watching her. Every time

she'd put her fingers to her lips, flames of desire had, in turn, licked at his loins. The woman was dangerous, and she didn't even know it. Not that he hadn't asked for every moment of agony by insisting she come and see Fremont in person.

Brian cursed to himself. The idea of using a dog like Fremont had been slow in taking hold, but now he really believed he could be more independent with a canine companion. As far as he was concerned, it was time to get back into life, and Fremont's failure to help as expected was a hard blow. It had taken a lot of courage to call Molly, but Brian saw the act as absolutely necessary for his ultimate survival. At this point, he'd do whatever he had to do to gain the total independence he'd only dreamed of before.

Molly hadn't missed the fact that Brian was watching her the way a cat watched a mouse hole. She'd expected as much. Yet there seemed also to be a kind of quiet desperation in his expression. It was obvious he loved Fremont, even though the dog was letting him down.

Not only that, she reasoned, Fremont was letting down FFI and all it stood for. She couldn't allow that to happen. No dog she'd ever placed had been returned for lack of enthusiasm, least of all a Labrador retriever.

They were big, good-natured clowns with hearts of gold. No. Something traumatic must have happened to cause the dog to behave so strangely, and the only way to get to the bottom of the problem was to be there to carefully watch the interaction between Brian and the dog.

She served Brian another piece of pizza, then wiped her hands on the napkin he quickly thrust at her. "Thanks. You know, I've been thinking." When he made no comment, she went on. "The only way I can get to the heart of what's wrong will be to observe you two together."

"I thought that was what you were doing now."

"I am. It's just not enough."

"Oh." Tipping up his soda can, he drained it and held it out. "Want another?"

"No. Thanks. I'm fine." She got to her feet. "I have to be going, but I'll be back."

Brian saw no reason to argue. They'd managed to eat nearly a whole pizza without leaping into each other's arms, so perhaps the danger had passed. Not that he believed that for a instant. However, as long as Molly was preoccupied with Fremont's problems and he was smart enough to keep his distance, he was sure they'd be fine. If she returned the following evening, he'd at least have had a whole day in which to convince himself to leave her alone. Surely he could manage that.

"All right," he said, escorting her to the door. "Do whatever you think will help. I'm really desperate here."

Her voice and eyes softened. "I know you are. And this apparent failure matters to me, too. It's not only a reflection on my training, it's a blow to my pride. My dogs don't fail."

Rather than shake her hand and take the chance of touching her again, Brian merely nodded as he bid her good-night. At the sound of her van pulling away, he let out his breath in a noisy whoosh. Well, that was that. He'd made it through her visit and not once embarrassed himself, at least not so that anyone would notice but him.

Shifting his body in the chair, he tried not to think of Molly. Finding that impossible, he went to clean off the table. Fremont was still sitting next to the place Molly had vacated.

"Yeah, boy, I miss her, too," Brian confessed. "Come on. There's one piece of pizza left. I'll put it in your dish for you."

Head down, the Lab followed. As soon as he'd eaten the pizza and his regular dinner besides, he lay down to watch Brian, his head resting on his outstretched paws.

Brian piled the clean dishes from the dishwasher with the others on the counter. The cupboards he used to use were now out of his reach. He'd been so busy at boot camp, he'd not had time to rearrange his kitchen. Sam and Joyce had emptied most of the upper storage areas for him, piling the glasses and crockery on the counters, but Brian hadn't yet figured out where he was going to store them on a regular basis.

He looked at Fremont and snorted derisively. "You're sure I'm not disturbing you? Mind if I get a little work done?"

The dog merely blinked.

"Okay, then watch where I put all this stuff so you can get it for me when I need it."

The irony of Brian's comment seemed lost on Fremont. Opening all the doors below the tiled counter, Brian turned on the radio to a soft-rock station for background noise and went to work. The activity didn't take his mind off Molly as he'd hoped, but at least he was accomplishing something.

It was nearly an hour later when he heard a loud knock and went to answer the door. Fremont had gotten up a few moments before and headed for the living room. Until the knock, Brian had assumed the dog merely wanted to be let out.

Fremont woofed.

"Well, open the door, dummy. Go ahead.

I dare you." To his amazement, the dog put his mouth over the soft rubber covering with which Brian had equipped the knob, worked it around and actually did release the latch. Obviously pleased with himself, he wiggled all over and raced back to his master.

"Holy . . ." Brian stared as the door opened wider. There on his doorstep stood Molly Evans, a pillow in one hand, a small, blue overnight bag in the other. Her hair was windblown in spite of her French braid, and she had a wide, impish grin on her face.

"I'm back!"

"I can see that. The question is why." Although he was sure he knew, he couldn't make his mind accept the conclusions he'd come to.

"I told you. I'm going to observe you and Fremont."

Dear God, she sounded as excited as a kid going on her first camp out. Brian scowled. "I thought you were coming back tomorrow."

"Of course, I will. Tomorrow and every other spare moment, till I figure out what's gone wrong." Cocking her head, she studied his stormy expression. "You said to do whatever I thought would help. Well . . ."

"I didn't mean I was ready to take in boarders," he countered. "This place isn't finished. I use one spare bedroom for a gym, and the other is full of junk."

"No sweat." She entered and shut the door behind her. "I didn't expect you to have an extra bed. That's why I brought my own pillow. I have blankets in the car, too, if you're short."

"I snore."

"So does Fremont, and I've slept through that before." Making her way to the overstuffed, beige leather couch, she tossed her pillow into the corner and set the overnight bag on the floor. "Don't mind me. Just go about your business."

"No way, lady. You can't stay."

"Why not?" She struck her familiar hands-on-hips pose.

"You just can't, that's all."

Molly peered at him out of the corner of her eye. "A person wouldn't think a big, strapping guy like you would be afraid of a girl like me."

"Now wait just a minute," he said, rolling up beside her. "I never said anything like that."

"You didn't have to. It's written all over your face."

"Oh, it is, is it? Well you'd better take more reading lessons, Ms. Evans, because all that's written on my face is a desire for solitude."

"Peace and quiet. Got it," Molly said. "I'll be so quiet, you'll never know I'm here."

"Molly, you don't know what you're suggesting. I —"

Speaking softly, she seated herself on the arm of the couch to bring herself to his eye level. "I do know. And although it may be a bit difficult for both of us, we are adults, and my presence *will* solve your problems. I'm sure of it."

"You're not going to leave, are you?"

"Not unless you throw me out bodily, no," she said. "When I go to work tomorrow, you and Fremont can come with me."

"What good will that do?"

She shrugged. "It might shorten the time I have to act as your shadow."

"In that case, wake me in plenty of time," he said, starting for the hallway. "The sooner we get this headache over with, the happier I'll be. Stay there. I'll get you a blanket."

Molly managed to preserve her casual smile until he'd given her the blanket and left her alone in the living room. It was natural for him to want peace in his life. It just hurt to hear him say he'd be happy to be rid of her. She'd known that establishing herself under Brian's roof would be hard for her in a lot of ways, but she hadn't expected such a telling blow to her ego.

Spreading out the blanket, she fluffed her pillow and placed it at one end of the couch.

She hated the old feelings of childhood insecurity that surfaced whenever Brian acted cross with her, but she also knew she had those bad feelings to thank for giving her the courage to stay. A tender Brian Forrester was dangerous to her emotional health. A cross one she understood.

Chapter Eight

The first thing Molly heard the next morning was the rapid-fire click of Fremont's nails on the bare floor as he galloped toward her. Before she came fully awake, he'd bounded onto the couch, planted one foot in the middle of her stomach and was licking her face. In all the weeks she'd worked with him specially, even taking him home with her on occasion, he'd never acted so rowdy.

Fending him off with her hands as the blanket went flying, she yelled, "Oof! Get off me, you big lug! Fremont, down!"

He complied, wiggling in a circle in front of her and panting so fast, his lips were drawn back in what could be taken for a smile, if dogs smiled. Which they didn't, Molly reminded herself. It paid to remember that imagining a human personality for an animal was common but erroneous. In the case of a working dog, it could be disastrous.

"You're a *dog,* Fremont," she mumbled, tugging at her oversize, cotton-knit nightshirt. "Act like one."

In the background, Molly heard Brian's

warm laugh. Making a grab for the closest edge of the blanket, she pulled it to her chin, thought for a split second, then yanked it all the way up to lay over her face. She was more tired now than she had been when she'd gone to bed — or in this case, to couch. Her back had a kink in it, her neck was stiff, and she doubted she'd slept two of the six or so hours she'd laid there trying.

"It's six-thirty, Ms. Evans," Brian said, coming closer. "I've been up long enough to workout for half an hour and shower afterwards. Time to rise and shine."

"You shine, Forrester," she grumbled from beneath the blanket. "I'll rise, but that's all."

"Oh-oh. Maybe that's what I've been doing wrong," he said, chuckling to accentuate the disparity in their moods. "I'm cheerful in the morning. Maybe Fremont's used to a grump."

Molly lowered the blanket enough to expose only one eye. "Ugh. Morning. Give me an hour alone, okay?" Watching his expression change, she wasn't sure how to read it. Not knowing prickled her curiosity. Seeing his deep blue eyes darken prickled a lot more parts of her and she couldn't help wondering what it would be like to wake up to that smile and those stubble-shadowed cheeks every morning.

Nervous, she scooted back to sit up, taking

the blanket with her for modesty, and rubbed the soreness in the back of her neck. "Why are you staring at me like that?"

He didn't dare tell her she was the most beautiful sight he'd ever seen, with her childish nightshirt, sleepy eyes and thoroughly mussed yet lovely long hair.

"It's not you, it's me," he said, his voice less cheery, his smile fading. "Ever since the accident, I've been so glad to wake up at all, I can't understand how anyone can hate morning."

The confession took Molly by surprise. "I'd never thought of it quite that way."

"Well, do," he suggested. "You're alive, healthy, and you've got a lot more to be thankful for than I do. Try to remember that." He paused, running his hand over the day-old whiskers on his chin. "You know, that's not exactly true, what I just said about morning. At first I just wanted to die. Then I was angry most of the time. After a while, though, I came to the conclusion that life was better than the alternative."

"It took a while?"

"Yeah. A while." Wheeling away, Brian headed for the kitchen. "I'll go put on some coffee."

He'd realized, almost before the words were out of his mouth, that the basic change in his outlook had begun that fateful day when he'd met Molly in the elevator at the mall. She'd seemed so full of life, so upbeat and accepting of his condition, he'd finally started to accept it himself. Of course, he couldn't tell her that or she'd think he was making another pass, and Lord only knew where that would lead.

Looking down, he noted that Fremont was beside him. As Brian saw it, there were only two ways he was going to get Molly out of his life so she could at least have the opportunity to meet someone who was right for her. One, he'd have to give up Fremont, or two, he'd have to prove the dog *was* working well again.

Whatever happened, Molly mustn't stay long. His sanity was at stake, thanks to his suddenly recovered libido. More than that, he really liked her. The kindest thing he could do for her, as a friend, was to keep his hands off her and his heart in check so she never knew how much he'd begun to care.

Brian gripped the arms of the chair, looked at Fremont and gave him a command. To his amazement, the dog obeyed! Opening the cupboard Brian had indicated, the dog searched till his nose touched the coffee can.

"That's it. Get it. Hold!"

Fremont did. His strong jaws carefully closing around the can, he lifted it and brought it to Brian, depositing it in Brian's lap when he was instructed to.

Brian stared. "I'll be damned. Good boy!" Behind him he heard footsteps. Molly, still wearing her faded, teddy-bear-adorned shirt, had come into the room too late to see Fremont work. Brian was so excited, he told her immediately.

"Good," she said, clutching her street clothes and rubbing her eyes. "That probably means you won't need me around much longer." She yawned. "Mind if I take a shower?"

"No. Straight down the hall to your left. Clean towels are under the sink."

He quickly turned away so she couldn't see the intense emotional reaction he knew was written all over his face. The minute she'd mentioned not being around, his mood had plummeted. Damn it all, what was the matter with him? He knew there could never be anything permanent between them, so why was he always imagining himself with Molly? It had gotten so bad he could even see them together and —

The truth of his thoughts hit Brian like a sledgehammer crashing into his chest. He'd pictured Molly and himself together, all right, and every time it happened, he'd been standing on two feet. That was what made the picture right. And that was also why it could never be.

Fremont laid down on the floor beside Brian, stretched out and lowered his muzzle to his paws.

Molly's hair was a mass of tangles, thanks to her restless night. At home she had a dual-mirror system rigged up in her bathroom so she could look in one mirror and see the back of her head in another while she fashioned her French braid. Naturally, Brian's bathroom had no such arrangement.

She was beginning her third try at braiding neatly when he called to her.

"Hey, Evans. You awake in there? Breakfast is ready."

"I'm . . ." Molly made a face. "Oh, rats." The sections of hair fell from her fingers, and she opened the door to find him sitting outside, a questioning look on his face.

"You okay? I could have taken three showers in the time you've been in there."

"It's not the shower," she explained, pushing her fingers through her damp hair. "It's my braid. For some reason, I seem to be all thumbs today." And it isn't because you look so darned appealing in the morning, she added, only half believing the excuse.

"Your hair looks pretty like that," he said,

cursing himself for giving in to the urge to compliment her.

Molly blushed. "Thanks. It gets in the way though." Her color deepened. "At work, I mean."

"Yeah. Well, your eggs are getting cold. I scrambled them. Hope that's okay."

"You didn't have to cook for me."

"I know. But judging from the lunch you'd packed that day I came to FFI, you'd starve if somebody didn't feed you."

"I do okay." She knew she sounded defensive, but his concern had so touched her that she didn't dare respond the way she really felt. If she had, she might very well have cried. The last time she recalled either of her parents expressing such concern, she'd been a little girl. Later, when the family was in the process of disintegrating, it was her older sister and brother who'd taken over her care. Hardly more than children themselves, they'd had plenty of their own troubles to occupy their minds and very little time for their baby sister.

"If I hadn't seen you in that white dress the night of graduation, I'd disagree," Brian said, leading the way back to the kitchen. *Shut up, Forrester,* he ordered. *How many mistakes are you going to make before you learn?*

"I wear it to all the graduations," Molly

said. "On my salary, I can't afford to shop much."

Brian took a pan from the stove, motioned her to the table and started dishing up the eggs. "Not on a hundred and twenty-five dollars per dog, you can't. Why doesn't FFI charge a fee that's fair to themselves?"

Laughing, Molly poured each of them coffee and joined him at the table. "Because each dog costs over ten thousand dollars to raise and train. Most of the people we help could never afford a fee like that."

"*How* much?" He nearly choked. "You're kidding." His gaze darted to Fremont, who, since getting the coffee can, had refused to do another blessed thing.

"Not at all. So you can see why I'm so intent on making the most of every animal."

"Boy, I guess." Adding cream to his coffee, Brian stirred and watched the brown-and-beige swirls of colors. "So you solicit donations?"

Caught with a mouthful of egg, Molly added. "Mmm, hmm. This tastes as good as it smelled." She swallowed and wiped her mouth with a napkin. "Donations are all that keep us going. That and our volunteers. They're great."

"And I'll bet that's why you haven't asked for a raise, isn't it?" Before she answered out loud, her eyes had told him he'd spoken the

135

truth. With the world so full of people whose lives revolved around salaries and promotions, it was damned refreshing to meet a true altruist.

"I get by," Molly said.

"And you drive that old van because you like it, right?"

"It gets me where I want to go."

"Someday it won't," Brian told her with assurance. "You can't neglect machinery forever, you know. It'll quit."

"So you can fix it for me while I'm here." She knew she was taunting him, but she had her reasons. The scowl he shot her was so intense, she wondered if she'd gone too far.

Molly shrugged, trying to appear more nonchalant than she felt. "Okay, okay. Don't have a tizzy. I just figured, since the motor's in the back and down low, you could reach it. That's all."

"And do what — hit it with a hammer?"

Looking him straight in the eye, she made a silly face. "How should I know. I don't understand cars."

"They're easier to figure out than dogs, that's for sure," Brian said, casting a disgusted glance at the recumbent Fremont.

Molly checked her watch. They still had nearly forty-five minutes before she had to be at work.

Noting her action, Brian asked, "You late for a hot date or something?"

"No. I was just looking to see if I had time to fiddle with my hair again."

Brian watched her toss her head and flip her long hair back behind her shoulders. Every time she'd bent forward to take another bite of her breakfast, more of the fine, brown strands had slipped forward to caress her cheeks, and he could see how it would be difficult to work under those conditions. It might even be dangerous if she got it caught in something.

"I had a horse when Sam and I were kids," he said.

Raising one eyebrow, Molly finished her coffee. "And?"

"And, I used to braid its tail for shows and things. It can't be that much different to braid your hair."

She had to laugh. "Hopefully, it's a lot different."

"The texture would be, of course, but I'm really pretty good at braiding."

"I have a set of mirrors I use at home," Molly said, getting up to clear the table. "Then I can see what I'm doing." It also didn't help to know Brian was close by when she tried to keep her trembling hands steady enough to fashion the braid, but she declined to mention that small fact.

"Want me to give it a try?"

"No. That's okay. If worse comes to worst, I'll just tie it back into a ponytail." She bent to look under the sink. "Where do you keep the dish soap?"

"I don't wash anything in the sink," he said. "It's too hard to reach. I leave everything there, then run the dishwasher later."

"Not if you're at work with me, you won't," Molly reminded him. "Really, I don't mind doing this. After all, you fed me, and egg sticks to plates something awful if you don't get it off right away."

"Is *that* what that orange glue was?"

"Probably, although not having seen it, I can't say for sure." She smiled over at him. "How about cleanser? Do you have some of that to clean the sink with?"

Grinning back at her, Brian said, "Clean the sink? Why? Is it dirty? Beats me. I can't see the bottom without working at it."

"Okay, okay. I'll make do with laundry detergent." The sheepish look on Brian's face was so comical, she laughed.

"Joyce has been doing my laundry," he confessed. "I told you I wasn't all moved back in yet. I have bath soap, hand soap and shampoo, plus that gooey blue stuff for the dishwasher. Take your pick."

"Gooey blue, definitely," Molly said, reaching for the bottle. "Go get ready to leave. I'll take care of this."

While she busied herself in the kitchen, Brian took her advice and went to the bathroom to shave. Molly's hairbrush and comb were on the counter along with the rest of her toilet articles and that ridiculous T-shirtlike nightdress with the faded picture of a smiling teddy bear on the front. Thank goodness she wasn't a neatness freak, he thought, plugging in his electric razor. At least she wouldn't be hard to live with.

That thought stopped his heart. Molly had only spent one night under his roof and already he'd begun to get used to having her around. Brian lectured himself on the futility of such ideas while he shaved, then unplugged his razor and rolled up the cord. He sighed. The whole room smelled of freshness, shampoo and the special, sweet scent that was uniquely Molly.

His hand brushed over her nightdress. Lifting it, he brought it closer. Chances were she'd chosen to wear such a loose, nondescript garment because she thought it would make her less appealing. In his eyes, that was impossible. Molly was Molly, regardless of what she wore. No matter how much time passed, he knew he'd always be able to conjure up her image in the house, now that she'd actually lived there. However few sweet memories she left, they'd have to be enough to give him solace.

Laying aside the shirt, he gathered up her brush and comb. It wasn't truthful to lead her to believe all he wanted to do was help, but there was so little time to make the beautiful, lasting memories he coveted, so few genuinely honest excuses to touch her without making it seem as if he were making romantic advances, that he decided he had to act.

Molly had finished the dishes and was letting Fremont out into the enclosed backyard when Brian returned. She noticed her brush in his lap. As a child, she'd hated having anyone else brush her hair and once had gone so far as to cut her locks herself as a way of eliminating the problem. Her mother had been furious.

"Sit down at the table like you were," he said. "Give me a shot at the braid. I'll bet you'll be surprised."

"I don't like anyone fiddling with my hair," she said. "I have a very tender scalp."

His eyes darkened and his voice became husky. "I won't hurt you, Molly. I'd never hurt you."

Something in his expression told her how important it was to him to be able to offer her some kind of assistance. Without further argument, she did as he'd requested. When he closed the distance between them and came up behind her, she shuddered in anticipation of his touch.

Slowly, gently, he began to draw the brush down the length of her hair. His hand followed, smoothing, caressing, again and again until she closed her eyes in contentment. Brian's hands were large and strong, but his touch was that of a cautious, caring lover. Molly shivered all the way to her toes.

"Are you cold?" He stopped brushing and laid one hand on her shoulder.

It was all she could do to answer, all she could do to keep from turning around and falling into his arms. "No. I'm fine. It just tingles, that's all."

"I told you it wouldn't hurt."

She nodded. Oh, it hurt, all right. It hurt plenty, only her hair had nothing to do with it. Being touched with harshness, as she had been when her mother or sister had tended to her hair out of duty, was nothing like this. The more she was around Brian Forrester, the more of her childhood monsters he banished. It was those monsters, those fears, on which she'd balanced her life. Much more tenderness from him and she'd be so out of kilter, she might never get her emotions back on an even keel again.

"We're running out of time," Molly said, altogether more breathless than she liked.

His "I know" sounded just as intense. Neither of them was talking about her hair, and Molly knew it. So did Brian, she was certain, yet he'd done nothing out of the ordinary, nothing that could be construed as anything other than simple friendship.

Laying aside the brush, he sectioned her hair and began to braid. Molly could tell he wasn't doing it the way she would have, but she'd not have corrected him if her life had depended on it. Whatever he did, however her hair turned out, she'd wear it that way proudly. Appearances were not nearly as important as preserving Brian's pride of accomplishment.

He was almost done. His hands folded the last few sections, and Molly heard him sigh. Barely breathing, she didn't move. Wisps of loose hair at her nape tickled as his breath fanned them. Holding very still, she waited for his kiss. It never came. Instead, he handed the end of the braid to her over her shoulder.

"Here. I forgot to bring a rubber band."

"Thanks." As she grasped the braid, her fingertips brushed the backs of his fingers and he withdrew, rapidly and silently.

"You were right," he said, cynicism heavy in his words.

"I was?" Molly got to her feet, a bit surprised when her rubbery legs actually supported her.

"Yeah." He'd already crossed to the hall and was on his way into the living room. "It wasn't a bit like doing the horse."

"Thank goodness." Trying to be flippant, she failed to get the usual quick retort from him and was so nervous about it, she felt like giggling. "Maybe tomorrow I should whinny for you."

"By tomorrow I'll have bought you a bigger mirror," he countered. "Come on. We'd better get going or we'll be late."

Fremont was so excited about the prospect of going out with them that he fetched his FFI backpack the first time Brian sent him for it. Molly stood back and watched. Everything seemed to he fine between man and dog. If she hadn't seen Fremont balk with her own eyes, she wouldn't have believed it had happened at all.

Gathering up her purse and keys, Molly went to the door. "I'll move my van out of the way so you can get to the Austin more easily."

Brian was checking the straps on the harness

that held the pack. "We'll be there in a minute." He glanced up to be sure she was gone before tugging on his clothing to make room for his "problem." Hell, he hadn't even been looking at her, this time. If things kept on as they had been, pretty soon he'd be staying hard the whole damn day.

He looked down at Fremont, all decked out in the orange-and-green pack. The dog was panting, his mouth wide open, his brown eyes twinkling.

"What are you grinning about?" Brian demanded. "You started this whole mess."

Fremont woofed.

"Yeah, I know. It was dumb to touch her hair like that. I did it in a weak moment."

"Did what?" Molly asked, appearing back on the porch.

Brian blushed and concentrated on the dog. "Got Fremont" he ad-libbed. "I thought you were leaving."

"I was." Shrugging her shoulders, she made a disgusted face. "My van won't start."

"I warned you."

"You jinxed me, that's what you did. Do you suppose I could hitch a ride with you?"

"In a two-seat sports car? What about Fremont?"

"Oh." Molly was chagrined. Following Brian down the ramp and over to the driveway, she looked at the red Austin. There was a small space behind the seats that wasn't taken up when he loaded his chair. "I could hunker down back there," she suggested, pointing.

"No!"

"Well, you don't have to get mad. It was just an idea."

"A lousy one. There's no seat belt back there, Molly. Have you forgotten how I got like this?"

In truth, she'd forgotten he was even in a wheelchair, but it didn't seem like the best time to mention it. "Well, I can't take Fremont's seat, and you have to drive, so I guess I'm stuck."

"I'll make two trips," Brian said. "It isn't far. Take Fremont back into the house for now and I'll run you to work."

"Couldn't he sit on my lap if we put the belt around both of us?"

He considered for a moment. "The old human system is still in place. If you think you can stand his weight on your lap, it might be okay, but I won't take him without his safety restraints, either."

"Good. That makes me even more sure you're perfect for him. Too many pet owners are lax."

"Don't start that pet business again. I told

you, I don't want a pet."

"Sorry. A slip of the tongue."

Going around to the passenger side of the car, she let Brian put Fremont in and hook him up before she scooted in beside the excited dog. There was room for them both, if neither insisted on hogging the center of the seat.

"If you can still shift, this will work fine," Molly said. "He's sharing the seat with me."

Brian got himself in and stowed the chair. Reaching into a pocket in the side of his door he withdrew Fremont's driving goggles and slipped them on, threading the blue elastic band past the dog's floppy ears.

Only by clamping her hand over her mouth could Molly keep from laughing. When she'd warned Brian about possible damage to the dog's eyes, she'd not envisioned having him decked out like a 1920's race-car driver. All that was missing was the leather helmet!

Obviously proud, Fremont sat upright and faced front, his big, pink tongue lolling merrily as Molly put her sunglasses on. "You don't have goggles for everyone, I see," she quipped.

"Buy a pair and I'll take you for a ride more often," Brian shot back. "Lock your door."

"Yes, Captain. Ready to blast off."

Without further delay, Brian started the car and away they went. Molly, who was used to sitting much higher in her van, felt as if her rear end was about to drag the ground. She gripped the handle on the dash.

"Oh, my! It does give you a feeling of speed, doesn't it?"

"And power," Brian shouted over the noise of the engine and the wind. Glancing past Fremont, he laughed at Molly's tenseness and arched eyebrows. "You'll get used to it."

"My brother had a skateboard once. He used to push me on it. That's what this reminds me of."

Ignoring the comparison of his dream car with a mere skateboard, Brian downshifted. "I didn't know you had a brother."

"I don't see him very often," she said flatly. "My sister, either."

"Why not? Sam and I have a great time together, even now."

"Some folks are family oriented and some are not," Molly explained. "My family's never been close."

"Not even your parents? That's a shame." Brian couldn't imagine growing up in a situation like that.

She peeked over at him past Fremont's backpack. "Not really. It's helped me to be lots more independent. I prefer it that way."

Quiet, he thought about what she'd said. "No wonder you didn't want to promise me you'd stop working so hard and get out and have more fun."

"Now you're beginning to understand."

"And you don't mind being alone?"

"Not at all," she lied, close to tears behind the dark screen of her sunglasses. Her answer had been the truth up until recently. The reason for her change of heart was piloting the Austin expertly through traffic, oblivious to her private agony. Until she'd glimpsed what it could be like to be special to someone, until she'd opened her heart and made Brian Forrester the center of her soul, she'd never dreamed such things were possible for mere mortals.

Her feelings didn't alter reality, of course. Black was still black, white was still white, and marriage was still for fools. The problem was, for the first time in her life, Molly was sorry it was so.

Chapter Nine

"Wait over there under the trees, so you're in the shade, and just watch me work this golden retriever," Molly told Brian.

"What good will that do?"

"We always let the dogs observe others learning commands," she said. "They seem to pick up a lot that way."

Unconvinced, he did as she asked. Keith and Jim were also working with young dogs, and Brian could readily see why Molly was so tired at night. The training was repetitious, the dogs strong and stubborn. Typical of adolescents of any species, they wanted mostly to play.

He looked down at Fremont. The glossy black lab was in a relaxed pose, but Molly was right, the dog was actually watching the show.

By the time several hours had passed and it was time for Molly's break, Brian was eager to see what Fremont would do for him. He wasn't disappointed. With a few minor corrections, the dog performed beautifully; so well, in fact, that Brian decided to take him shopping instead of spending the whole day at FFI.

"I'll come back for you later," he told Molly. "What time do you get off tonight? Six again?"

"Yes. But you don't have to bother. I want to go home and pick up some clean clothes, anyway, and Keith lives just off Valley Parkway, too. He can drop me."

"We're practically neighbors," Brian said, surprised.

"Now that you're living in your own house, yes," she said. "When I'm done at home, I'll trot up the hill to your place. Can't be more than four or five miles, even if it is in a classier neighborhood. It's not really too far for me to walk."

"At night? Alone?" Brian's voice rose. "No way, lady. I'll be back this evening, pick you up here, take you to your house and wait for you. And in the meantime, I'll have your van looked at."

"It's not really necessary to go to all that trouble."

"Maybe not," he grumbled, "but I do have to do something to get that relic out of my driveway. It'll ruin my reputation."

"As a lothario?" Molly teased. "I should think having overnight guests would help."

"Not the female company, the car." He

lowered his voice. "And while we're at it, how come ol' Keith didn't know you'd moved in with Fremont and me?"

She blanched. "You didn't tell him that, did you?"

"That you showed up on my doorstep bag and baggage? No. He seemed so confused, I made excuses and shut up." One eyebrow arched, and Brian leaned closer. "You *are* with me in an official capacity, aren't you?"

Molly's white cheeks turned pink. "In a manner of speaking." She could tell from the expression on his face that more explanation was necessary before he'd drop the subject. "I — uh — decided to sleep over on my own."

"I take it it's not common practice."

"No. Not even close." By now her blush had extended to the roots of her hair, and she felt much too warm all over.

"Then, why?" He watched her chew on her lower lip before she answered. If she said she'd acted because she was romantically interested in him, he'd have to insist she leave. Although it was the last thing he wanted, it was the only fair — safe — thing to do.

"Because it's the best and fastest way to end the suspense and agony," she finally said.

Brian was about to remind her of her vow to remain unmarried, and thereby embarrass them both unnecessarily, when she clarified her statement.

"If Fremont is truly no good, you need to find out before you become any more attached to him and he to you. A clean break, soon, will be the kindest step if it turns out that's what has to happen. We all have to know — soon."

"I see." Brian took a deep breath and nodded. "Are you jeopardizing your job for me?"

Her smile was fleeting as she looked around to make sure no one else was close enough to hear. "Not if you don't blab about our becoming roommates."

"You should have warned me," he said quietly. "I'd never knowingly put you in hot water. You know that."

"I do know. It just hadn't occurred to me to mention the problems I might encounter if Claymore heard of my new training methods." She laughed. "I don't think they're in the manual."

"Probably not. So how do we explain your van in my driveway?"

"It broke down," Molly said. "That's the truth." Coloring more, she shot him an apologetic smile. "I really do hate to have to lie about anything."

"But sometimes it's for the best, isn't it?" Brian looked up at her, wondering if she sus-

152

pected how dangerous even the tiniest bit of truth between them was when it came to feelings. Keeping his mouth shut was the easy part. Keeping his emotions out of his expression was much harder. The love just seemed to leap from his soul into his eyes, and he knew it.

Preserving his self-control as best he could, Brian spoke to Fremont and turned to go. Molly followed.

"I'll have Sam or one of the mechanics take a look at your van for you," he said, holding up his hands as she started to protest. "Consider it an exchange of services for the extra training you're giving Fremont."

Molly wasn't sure that was really fair, but she had little choice. His people were experienced professionals, and she knew the van needed work. Besides, she wasn't exactly an amateur in her field. A trade of skills would solve her dilemma of how to pay for repairs, if they weren't too expensive.

"All right, if you insist. I left the keys on your hall table. Be kind to the poor old thing. It's got a lot of miles on it."

"How many?" he asked out of curiosity.

"About a hundred and thirty thousand, I think. The engine was replaced, though."

Brian was almost afraid to ask. "How long ago?"

"Oh, maybe three years."

"In miles, Molly. Time only counts in dog years and library fines."

"I don't know. Sixty thousand?" Judging from the shocked expression on his face as he paused and looked up at her, she figured he'd go home, dig a big hole and bury her old van right where it sat.

Brian wheeled away, talking to himself. Sixty thousand miles! Shoot, she was probably due for another engine replacement. No telling what was wrong with the van. On the way home, he'd swing by the shop and talk with Sam about taking on a charity case.

It wouldn't be the first time, and besides, he had a special interest in this one. Molly was a good, kind person whose talents could have led her to a job that paid lots more money than she was obviously making now, yet she'd chosen to work with the FFI dogs because she felt it was her solemn duty. Such sacrifice deserved reward. Even if he couldn't provide it personally, he was glad to be able to see that someone else did.

After seeing Sam, he'd stop at the grocery store and a motorcycle shop. He needed soap, cleanser, something good for dinner and another pair of goggles just like Fremont's. If Molly was going to tease him about not providing eye protection for all his passengers, she was going to have to live with the results of her taunts.

Brian grinned. Red. He'd get her a red pair to match the car.

"I don't know where he is, Bev," Molly said, scanning the nearly empty parking lot from the window in her office. "I'm worried. He said he'd be here before six to get me. Something must have happened to him."

"Maybe you should telephone him."

"I tried. There was no answer."

"Then call his brother. Wasn't Brian planning to go talk to him when he left here?"

"I think so. He was going to ask Sam to look at my van."

Bev handed her the phone and began to dial the number in the FFI file. Knowing she had to do something, Molly held the receiver to her ear. Because she had met both Sam and Joyce, it wouldn't he like talking to strangers. Still, she didn't want to worry them unnecessarily. The voice that answered was a man's.

"Hello, Mr. Forrester? This is Molly Evans from FFI."

"Molly! Of course. How are you?"

"Umm, fine. I just wondered if you'd heard from Brian lately."

"Is something wrong?"

The poor man sounded worried, but she

didn't know how else to broach the subject. "I don't think so," Molly said. "It's just that he'd promised to pick me up and he's late. I thought maybe he was with you."

"Ah, I see." Sam made a chortling noise.

"What's so funny?" Molly was too concerned to share in his good humor without hearing an explanation of it first.

"Hopefully, Brian is what's funny," Sam said. "You see, I pulled a nasty trick on him, and I'll bet he's up to his elbows in grease. In the old days, he used to lose all track of time when he got to tinkering with an engine."

"An engine?" She shared Sam's excitement. "Mine?"

"That's my guess."

"Oh, that's wonderful. I was so hoping he'd get out and at least try to work at what he liked best. Even if it's harder, it'll be good for him."

"So are you," Sam said. "I've never seen Brian so enthused — or so cranky."

"The bad moods are to be expected," she explained. "He just needs time. How did you ever get him to agree to work on my van? He told me he couldn't do it."

Sam laughed again. "I let him think we were real shorthanded and behind schedule. Then I said if he'd just take a look at the van ahead of time, I'd come and help as soon as I was free."

"And you didn't?"

"Nope. I figured he'd look a bit, then fiddle with it and before long, he'd be totally engrossed, once he got started."

The only concern Molly had was whether Brian was all right. "He can't get hurt, can he?"

"Not unless he tries to replace the engine by himself."

"Could he?" Now she was really getting worried. If Brian was injured working on her van, she'd never forgive herself.

"Of course not. At least not in the middle of his driveway." Sam paused. "You said he stood you up. Do you need a ride somewhere? I can come get you if you like."

"No, thanks," Molly said. "A colleague of mine has offered. Besides, you need to stay away from Brian. By now, he's probably good and mad at you."

"*That's* the truth. And Molly . . ."

"Yes."

"Thanks for caring."

"Our students always come first at FFI," she said.

"Molly?"

"Yes?"

"Bull."

The remark was made with such good humor and kindness, she couldn't take offense. "We only train canines here, Mr. Forrester. If you want bovines, you'll have to contact a cattle ranch."

"No need," Sam said, chuckling. "I get enough bull from my brother to keep me well supplied."

She found herself smiling as he spoke. "He's lucky to have you."

"That's what families are for."

"I repeat, he's lucky to have you."

"And to have you," Sam told her. "You didn't know him before the accident, but I did. Since meeting you, he's more like the old Brian we all knew and loved."

"I'm glad. I told him that a service dog would make a difference in his outlook. It always does."

"The dog is nice," Sam agreed, "but it's you he talks about all the time."

"Me? Really?" She gripped the receiver more tightly.

"Yes." Hesitant, Sam cleared his throat. "Look, Molly, I know I shouldn't get involved, but I'm afraid my brother is worrying so much about what's best for you, he's overlooking what might be best for himself."

Dreading the thought Sam might be right, Molly sat down and waited for him to go on.

"He says he feels like a man when he's with you."

"I've never seen him as anything else," she confessed.

"That's the point. Has he told you about his past? About Pam?"

"Some."

"Well, she did more of a job on Brian than the accident did. By the time she was through with him, I wondered if he'd ever recover."

"It's understandable. He loved her." Saying the words was harder than Molly had imagined it would be. Thinking of Brian holding and making love to another woman caused her actual physical pain.

"Maybe. Both Brian and Pam were deluded, if you ask me. They were playing the parts society had given them — she was a glamorous, polished career woman, and he was the daring, well-to-do designer and builder of classic cars whose social status she'd decided to elevate by judicious use of his money. Before he knew it, she'd have had him all decked out in business suits all the time, moved to Rancho Santa Fe or Del Mar and hobnobbing with her chosen circle of friends."

Molly couldn't believe Brian would have been so blind. "I hardly think he'd have done any of that if he didn't want to."

"Maybe he and Pam would have broken up

even if there hadn't been an accident. I don't know. I do know that the first time Brian came home with grease under his nails from working, she'd have pitched a fit and told him he wasn't refined enough."

Molly puffed the air out of her lungs with a *humph*. It was ridiculous to imagine Brian living a life like the one Sam had described. He was too dynamic, too intelligent, too stubborn and too . . . wonderful. Why anyone would want to change him was beyond her.

"You can help him, Molly," Sam said. "You already have."

"How?"

"Just continue to be yourself. He needs a woman like you."

"But —"

Sam interrupted. "Look, I'm sorry if I embarrassed you. I just thought, if I filled you in about his past, it might help you deal with his future."

"It's all right," she said, managing to sound noncommittal about anyone's future. "If he calls, tell him I caught a ride home and I'll talk to him later."

"Okay. If you see him first and he's steamed at me, remind him that I love him, will you?"

"Sure." Molly bid Sam goodbye and hung up the phone. She'd be glad to give Brian the message. All she had to do was make sure she didn't blush when she spoke the words.

Molly's mind echoed Sam's sentiments. She didn't have to say it to know it. Warm, tender feelings for Brian Forrester had grown to immense proportions in a secluded corner of her heart while she'd constantly denied their existence. Concern had become fondness; fondness had become love. It would remain her secret, of course. She loved him too much to ever tell him.

"She's where?" Brian demanded. "Well, why didn't you go get her for me?"

Sam told him he'd offered and been turned down. "So she let that twerp, Keith, drive her? Terrific."

"She didn't say who was taking her home," Sam cautioned. "And don't jump all over me about it. *I'm* not the one who left her stranded."

"You left *me* stranded."

"That's another story. I did it for you."

"I figured as much." Brian thought for a moment. "She told me she lives somewhere near Valley Parkway. Did she give you her address?"

"No. I thought you'd have it."

"Well I don't. Her phone number, either. If she's not in the book, I'm stuck."

"She'll call you, little brother. Molly's a nice girl."

"Yeah," Brian agreed. "She also drives me crazy." He grimaced at Sam's ribald laugh. "It's not funny. I end up running around acting like some randy teenager in heat. It's not a pretty sight." The laugh on the other end of the line grew so loud, Brian held the receiver away from his ear. "Shut up, Sam."

"Have you told her?"

"Hell, no. I've spent most of my time trying to keep her from guessing."

"That's dumb."

Brian sobered. "It's necessary. Molly's too good for me."

"On that point, I agree," Sam said. "But don't you think she deserves a chance to decide that on her own?"

"She's already decided," Brian told him. "Marriage is not on her agenda."

"Yet, you mean."

"Ever, as far as I'm concerned. If she did decide to give up her single life, she could certainly do better than me."

"That's actually debatable." Sam was still chuckling. "While you were busy complaining, I grabbed the phone book and found an M. Evans. You interested in the number?"

Brian grabbed a pencil. "Yeah. Shoot. And stop that idiotic laughing. You sound like the automated clowns outside a carnival fun-house."

Molly's phone rang ten times before she answered.

"Thank God," Brian said. "I was about to give up."

"I gave up an hour ago and came home," she said. "Did you take a nap and oversleep?" His loud reaction told her Sam had guessed right.

"Sleep! I was working. On your van, if you must know."

Thrilled, Molly grinned so wide, her cheeks hurt. "So is it terminal? Do I jack up the radiator cap, as my father used to say, and drive a new car under it?"

"Volkswagens are air-cooled, Molly. No radiator. And, yes, it's bad. You really need a whole new engine."

"I need a whole new car, right?"

"It might be more sensible."

She sighed. "Speaking of sensible, how's Fremont?"

"Dumpy. He misses you, I think. He did help me a little today, though. I dropped a crescent wrench and he picked it up for me. Had to crawl part way under the van to do it, too."

"That's great!"

"He thought so, too. Danced all over in a puddle of oil and I had to banish him to the backyard till it wears off his paws."

She couldn't help but laugh at the comical description. "Since it was my oil, I'll help you clean him up. Be there in fifteen minutes or so."

"Wait! Tell me how to get to your house and I'll come and get you."

"That's really not necessary. It won't be dark for half an hour or so."

"Humor me."

She did. When she'd finished her directions, he asked if she'd eaten.

"No, why?"

"Because I'm starved, and I never did get to the grocery store the way I'd planned. Where would you like to go for dinner?"

"That's not necessary, either. We can stop and get steaks and barbecue them here, if you want."

"You're asking me over to your house?" Brian knew she had, yet his logical side insisted on further proof.

"Unless you don't want to come."

"No! I do, I do. Don't go anywhere. I'll be there in a few minutes."

Molly was still grinning to herself when she heard his car drive up. When they'd talked, he'd sounded like a kid on Christmas morning

164

who'd just seen the gift he'd asked for under the tree. She looked around her small living room. It was cluttered but clean, just the way she'd pictured Brian's house to be before he and Pam had torn it up to redecorate.

He'll like it here, Molly thought. He'll fit. And I'll like having him. A pleasant peace descended over her, transcending a lot of the nervousness she'd felt anticipating his arrival. Smiling more broadly, she went to the door to greet him.

Chapter Ten

"Hop in," Brian called to her from the driveway. "It'll be easier if I stay in the car and we go buy dinner first."

Molly grabbed her purse, slammed the front door behind her and bounded down the steps. "Good idea." Her brow wrinkled as she stared at the vacant spot next to Brian. "Where's Fremont?"

"The oil, remember? He'll survive a couple of hours alone in my backyard." As Molly got into the car and fastened her seat belt, he handed her a small, white plastic sack.

"What's this?"

"For you," Brian said. "Open it."

Cautiously, she bent to peer into the bag. If he'd already progressed to the point at which he was buying her gifts, she knew she'd either have to refuse to accept or chance letting him think their relationship had deepened too much.

Her eyes widened. Instead of candy, flowers or jewelry, the bag contained a bright red pair of goggles. She lifted them out. "How did you know my size?"

Brian laughed as he took them from her, reached up and slipped the band over her head. "They're adjustable. You were so jealous of Fremont's pair, I bought you your own."

Modeling them for him, she felt both foolish and elated. It was good to share such silliness with a friend like Brian. "Do they do me justice?" she asked, laughing.

"No," he said, "but then, neither do those FFI T-shirts you wear all the time."

"At least I'm color-coordinated tonight," Molly noted. "I wore the red one."

"Do you have any other clothes?"

"You don't like how I dress?"

Backing out of the short driveway into the street, Brian shrugged. "Well . . . ."

"Thanks a lot." Feigning anger, she folded her arms across her chest.

"I'd think you were beautiful if you were draped in nothing but a sheet," he said honestly. "It just seems a shame that you don't make the most of your natural attributes."

"Flattery will not, I repeat, *not* get me to drape myself in a bed sheet for you, Mr. Forrester, so don't go getting any such ideas."

"The teddy-bear shirt is the worst," he said, careful to keep his eyes on the road and off Molly.

"My teddy? I thought men liked teddies."

Chuckling, he signaled, then turned into the market parking lot. "I believe you have your bears mixed up, Ms. Evans. The teddies I like are made of satin and lace."

"I wonder what color." Molly remarked quietly to herself. If Brian hadn't shut off the engine of the Austin at precisely that moment, he wouldn't have heard her. She hadn't intended that he answer. The question was more a subconscious wish that his personal experiences with his former fiancée hadn't been so pleasant. So intimate. So memorable.

Placing one arm over the back of Molly's seat, he cupped her shoulder, slipped his thumb under the neckline of her shirt and brushed his thumb over her clavicle. "It doesn't matter, Molly. You've shown me that the outside of a person is secondary. So is clothing."

For a few seconds she was transfixed, frozen in place and time. Then she smiled at him. "Secondary or not, I believe I'll keep mine on, if you don't mind."

"Spoil sport."

She opened the car door. "You coming?"

"No. I've had a rough afternoon. You just pick something good, and I'll eat it with no arguments."

"That'll be the day," she quipped, climbing out of the car. "In case you haven't noticed, we argue about everything."

"Not really."

"We do so. See?" Molly grabbed her purse and turned away, laughing lightly. It was good to be with Brian. Too good. She felt as if she were on a thrilling amusement-park ride, thoroughly enjoying herself, yet knowing the ride would soon end. Such was life, she told herself. Nothing external ever lasted. That was why it made perfect sense to depend totally on oneself.

Dodging two little boys who had decided the slickly waxed store aisles made a great place to run and slide, she pushed her cart up to the meat counter, methodically chose two T-bone steaks and moved on. Teddies, indeed. Did he actually think she'd wear one of those torturous garments just for him?

Molly blushed, picturing herself clad in the satin and lace he'd described. Why, she didn't even own such impractical clothing. And if she did, it wouldn't matter. No way was she going to partially disrobe in front of Brian.

But she had, she realized. Oh, sure, her nightshirt covered her body and half her thighs. Still, she had been stark naked beneath it.

A sudden flash of warmth and excitement came over her. Tonight she would sleep in his house once more. What could it hurt to at least wear a gown that didn't look as though it doubled as a dust rag? Sam had sworn her influence had made Brian feel like a man again. Surely it would bolster his ego further if she dressed more to his liking. It wasn't much to ask.

But would it be safe? As she pitched a bag of potato chips into her basket, she chided herself for doubting Brian's promise that he would never hurt her. He wouldn't. They were friends now, and she knew he'd never do anything to jeopardize that friendship.

She and Brian Forrester would probably be lifelong buddies, Molly decided. If her wearing other, attractive clothing allowed him to more fully accept his physical limitations, then she owed it to him to do what she could to help. The hardest part would be stepping back, knowing she loved him, and watching him eventually move on to a permanent relationship with a more suitable woman. That was going to be a bummer. It would happen the moment the amusement-park ride was over.

She hoped it wasn't soon.

Brian had made himself at home in Molly's house, just as she'd expected. The barbecued steaks had been done to perfection, and they were seated at a picnic table under an ancient wisteria vine, eating, when she noticed that he didn't seem to be relishing the meal. "Is something wrong?"

"No." He glanced at the ramp from her back door to the lower level of the patio.

"I'm glad I had that built last summer," Molly remarked. "It makes it so much easier for you."

"Yeah. I thought maybe this house used to belong to an older person or something and that was left over."

"No. The ramp idea was all mine. This house is just a rental, but my landlord said he didn't mind as long as I didn't change the porch underneath it."

"Must make it a lot easier for you," Brian said.

"It does." She cut another bite of her steak. "This is delicious." While she watched, he seemed to come to terms with something, accepted whatever it was and began to eat. The next time he spoke, he'd polished off his T-bone.

"I'll bet they all appreciate your thoughtfulness."

"Who? I agree I'm a wonder, but I have no idea what you're talking about."

"Your guests," Brian said.

"My what?"

He gestured toward the ramp. "The other cripples you bring here. I'm sure they appre-

171

ciate the ease of access."

Molly's mouth gaped. "I ought to slug you for sounding so derogatory, but I'll let it slide — this time."

"That's big of you. Well, thanks for the meal. I'd better be going."

Launching herself across the space between their chairs, she grabbed his arm. "Hold it. You're not going anywhere."

"Why? Haven't you done enough for the poor victim yet? Trust me, Molly. Your good deed is complete. You can let me go now."

"Good deed? Is that what you think this is? Oh, for heaven's sake!" Pacing away, she turned back to face him. "If I weren't a lady, I'd, I'd . . ."

"You'd what?"

"Cuss, probably. What is the matter with you? We were getting along fine when you first got here. Why the change? What did I do to make you think my invitation was some kind of charity project?"

"It's pretty obvious," Brian said flatly. "Why would an able-bodied woman have her house renovated to accommodate wheelchairs unless she made a practice of inviting guys like me to visit?"

"Maybe because she trained dogs at home and sometimes used a chair to do it," Molly

172

countered. "Know what? I think you're jealous!"

"Don't be stupid." Brian's ears had begun to burn first. Now he could feel the crimson color infusing his entire face.

" 'Stupid'?" Molly repeated. "You want to see 'stupid'? Look in the mirror."

"Sure."

"Oh, crimony." She waved her arms into the air. "I don't know why I should tell you this, but you're the first student I've ever asked to dinner. There. Are you satisfied?"

"I wasn't jealous," Brian said, knowing it was a bald-faced lie, and rationalizing saying it because he didn't dare start telling Molly the truth. Once he began, he was afraid he'd say far too much.

He turned away from her. "I don't know what's the matter with me, Molly. I can be breezing along smoothly, enjoying myself, and all of a sudden I'm so angry, I can't see straight." Making a fist, he hammered it against the arm of his chair. "It's me I'm mad at, not you."

"I know." Closing the distance between them, she stood behind him and placed her hands on his shoulders, massaging the tense muscles. "I suppose it's a little like when we were children and wanted to do some of the things the bigger kids did, only when we tried, we failed."

She let her hands slide down to rest on his upper arms while she considered her next words. "For you, it would be as if you'd already been the older child, knew exactly what it was like to succeed, yet were reduced to the learning stage again."

"Worse," Brian said, his voice husky. "I'm no naive kid. I know I'll never be able to do the things I once did."

"I won't offer you platitudes," Molly told him as her fingers gently rubbed his arms through the thin fabric of his shirt. "I didn't know you before, but I know you now, and there's no doubt in my mind that you can accomplish far more than you give yourself credit for. You're strong, not just of body, but of heart. A man like you doesn't fail. He tries different ideas till he works around the obstacles in his path and eventually succeeds."

When Brian took one of her hands in his, she didn't resist. He raised her palm to cup his cheek, placed a kiss on her fingers, then clasped them tightly and drew them down to his chest, holding on the way a drowning man clings to a lifeline.

Still behind him, Molly leaned over, slipped her other arm around his neck and laid her cheek against his hair, kissing him gently.

She'd wait like that till he was ready to turn around rather than embarrass him. A cool breeze fanned them, and she hoped it would soon dry the few drops of moisture that had trickled onto her palm.

Brian Forrester was crying.

Brian realized Molly knew he'd disgraced himself, yet she'd not let on, and for that he blessed her a thousand times over. The strained atmosphere on the patio had long since passed. Molly was washing dishes while he dried them. Their attempt at cooperative domesticity seemed to he going quite well.

"Just like Ward and June Cleaver, aren't we?" Brian quipped.

"I was thinking more like Ma and Pa Kettle."

Brian chuckled and handed her the soggy towel. "In that case, I should be snoozing in my rocking chair. Pa never worked very hard."

"Except at producing children. Speaking of which," she said, trying to hide her blush and wishing she'd been more careful of the subject matter in her effort to make silly banter, "you should be getting home to Fremont. He's probably starving by now."

"Ah, yes, our little one. I think he takes after your side of the family."

"His intelligence, you mean?"

"No, his smile and good nature."

She grinned at him. "Thanks."

"You're welcome. Will you be going with me?"

"I should," Molly said. She sighed. "I just wish I knew why Fremont turns his good behavior on and off like a faucet. He's not normal."

"Like I said, he takes after you."

Molly whacked Brian with the dish towel and he ducked. Grabbing it, he wadded it into a tight ball and threw it at her. She ran into the living room, dodged to the opposite side of her floral-print Early American sofa and stood there giggling as be approached. "Déjà vu."

Brian stopped opposite her, the maple coffee table and couch between them. "No way, lady. I'm not diving off any more porches for you."

"Good. You could get hurt."

Making a pouting face, he raised his arms and pointed to the skin of his elbow. "I did. Right here."

The spot was barely red. "Doesn't look bad to me."

"Internal injuries," he insisted. "You should kiss it and make it better."

"Well . . ."

"It hurts a whole bunch."

"Okay." Cautiously, she circled the sofa and skirted the end of the low table. "You wouldn't kid me, would you?"

"Nope." Try as he might, Brian couldn't stifle the grin that spread across his face or the mischievous look in his eyes.

Molly balked, just out of reach. "I think it needs first aid, not a kiss." Darting through a doorway, she returned moments later with a paper-wrapped plastic bandage, opened it and stuck it to his elbow in the general vicinity of his supposed injury.

With a roar, Brian lunged for her, but she evaded him. He glanced at the bandage. It wasn't the usual flesh-tinted kind. Instead, it was decorated with brightly-colored animal pictures. "Bunnies?" he hollered. "You stuck little pink bunnies on me?"

Molly began to giggle. "Do you want to make your hurt all better or not?"

"Not if I have to wear a bandage with bunnies on it. Don't you have anything normal in this house?"

"I'm shocked at you, Mr. Forrester," she said, still chuckling between comments. "What's not normal around here?"

"Well, dog biscuits in the cookie jar, for one thing. I peeked. I was hoping for chocolate chip and I got Purina."

"One little eccentricity, and he besmirches

my housekeeping. Fine guest he is."

"One? How about the basket of squeaky toys in the bathroom? Or the squishy rubber covers on all the doorknobs?"

"You forgot the chewed up tennis shoes with cayenne pepper on them. They were especially made for the F litter."

"I missed those," Brian said. "They must be lots of fun to wear."

"I sacrificed them to the cause." Exhausted from her hard day and the tension of having Brian so near, Molly slid over the arm of the couch and sank into the cushions. "Want to watch some TV?"

"Yes, but I am a little worried about Fremont being home alone for so long. He'll be hungry, too. Shouldn't we be going?"

"I suppose so." Thinking about her earlier plans to please Brian by dressing differently, she dismissed the idea. If their latest mock battle was any indication, they were growing much too comfortable with each other. No use making things more complicated by exciting his male . . . tendencies. He was already quite enough man for any woman, especially her.

Molly picked up her purse from the hall table and headed for the door. "Tomorrow I'll drive my van to work so you won't have to bother with me. Then if Fremont continues to behave as well as he did today, I can leave you to the solitude you said you needed and start sleeping in my own bed again."

"Uh, right," Brian said.

She paused. "You did say you'd fixed my van, didn't you?"

"I said I worked on it. I don't recall claiming I'd repaired it."

"Well, how long will it take? I mean, can I begin to count on it in a day or so?"

Brian merely shrugged. "Beats me. Right now, it's a little under the weather."

"For instance?"

"Let's just say it's nonoperable, shall we?"

"Because it's still running rough?" she asked.

"Well, no." Leading the way to the Austin, he refrained from further comment until they were both seated in the car. Molly was staring at him, so he cleared his throat and smiled before explaining. "It's disassembled. You need new spark plugs, V-belts and at least a rebuilt fuel pump and filter. There's no sense putting it back together like it is."

"You killed my van?"

"It was already dead."

"It was sick."

"Terminally."

Sighing, she settled back in the seat. "What will I do without transportation? Oh, well, I suppose Keith —"

"You've got me," Brian interjected, slamming the car into gear. No matter what he did or said, Molly always kept coming back to her reliance on another man, and the idea was making him crazy. He decided to let her know how he felt. "You don't need Keith."

What I *don't* need is to spend more time with you, she thought, closing her eyes and letting her mind wander. Lately, it never wandered far from images of Brian Forrester. Besides being the sexiest man alive, he was fun to be with. His honesty and candor with regard to his innermost feelings had touched her. She'd be willing to bet a month's pay he'd not opened up like that to anyone else, not even Sam.

So what was she going to do? She certainly couldn't abruptly refuse to see him anymore. To do that would be to negate the progress he'd made, and what other choices did that leave her? Brian's assurances of his manhood and intrinsic worth seemed tied to her responses to him. Heck, she couldn't even mention Keith without drawing Brian's ire.

The solution seemed obvious. In order to successfully pull away without destroying him, she'd have to try to reinforce his self-image until it was strong enough to remain firm when she was gone. To do that, she'd have to convince him he was a whole man.

Molly's palms began to perspire; her mouth grew dry. It went against all her moral principles to do what she was thinking, yet how else could she convince him he was still a complete, virile lover? She swallowed hard. And what if he refused her? What if she offered him her body and he laughed at her feeble, untutored attempts at seduction?

That was what probably would happen, she rationalized. Surely she wouldn't have to go through with making love to him once he realized she was such a novice. It would be enough that she'd volunteered. After that, he was bound to be convinced he was attractive enough for any woman.

Chancing a surreptitious glance at Brian, Molly felt her stomach knot with desire. Of course, he would turn her down. And it would hurt more than she could imagine. It already did.

Chapter Eleven

Molly tried to ignore the various unidentifiable parts of her van that were lying in Brian's driveway as she followed him to his door. Temples throbbing, her head was still spinning with the portent of the dangerous idea she'd had on the way to his house. Whether or not she ever seriously considered implementing it, for the present, all she wanted to do was take two aspirins, curl up in her well-worn nightshirt and get some sleep.

Not that sleep would come easily, no matter how exhausted she was, but at least she'd have Fremont as a distraction and wouldn't spend every waking moment thinking about Brian.

He unlocked the door, opened it and cursed. Peering past him, Molly was speechless.

"Fremont!" Brian bellowed. "You're in deep —"

The big Lab trotted up to him, a tattered scrap of fabric in his mouth, his tail wagging. Molly recognized what was left of her teddy-bear shirt. She grimaced. Now, what was she going to wear to bed?

Brian pushed the dog's head off his lap and wheeled farther into the room. Several racing magazines lay in shreds on the floor, their form little more than glossy confetti. In the midst of the scraps was another piece of Molly's shirt.

She walked over, picked it up and held it out, recognizing the neck and part of one shoulder. "Well, I see he knows how to open the door by himself after all. Guess you didn't lock it."

"Not the back door. He was supposed to be guarding it."

"Maybe he did," she offered. "It's possible burglars entered, made this mess and then he bravely drove them off."

"Oh, right." Checking the kitchen and bedrooms, Brian was relieved to find no more damage, not even the oily paw prints he'd expected. By the time he returned to the living room, Molly had disciplined Fremont and had the mess almost cleaned up.

"You should have put cayenne paper on your shirt," Brian said. "I suppose you really liked it."

"As a matter of fact, I did." She balled up the cloth remnants with the magazine pages and tossed the whole armload into a nearby wastebasket. "Poor teddy. He never had a chance. Fremont must have sneaked up on him and *pow!* No more bear."

Brian hoisted the wastebasket. "We could have a funeral for him."

Laughing lightly, Molly shook her head. "Naw. Use him for a dust rag if you like, or take him out in the yard to wipe up the grease while you work on my van."

Brian made no reply. If he had his way and were sure she wouldn't laugh at him, he'd take the pieces of the shirt, put them aside and consider them a memento of time spent with Molly. God, he was going to miss that woman.

"I'll buy you another shirt," he said. "Come on. The mall closes at nine. We'll have to hurry."

"That's a nice offer, but not tonight," Molly said with a yawn. "Surely you must have *something* of yours I could wear. How about a T-shirt or one of those muscle shirts like you had on when I first met you?"

"They're not very warm."

Molly's initial thought was that being around Brian left her warm enough to abandon all clothing, but she refused to put that thought into words. Instead, she said, "I'll have a blanket. I'll be fine."

"Any particular color shirt?" he asked, starting for his room.

"I don't care. Just bring the longest one."

The brief look he shot back at her left her feeling already stripped bare. And then he was gone.

While Molly waited for Brian, she seated herself on the couch and took Fremont's head in her hands. Chocolate brown eyes gazed back at her with intelligence.

"You're going to have to shape up, old boy," she told the dog. "Or who knows what will happen to you. I'd take you myself, if I didn't have to bring other dogs home all the time."

Feeling a mental bond with the big Lab, she concentrated her thoughts and her energy, willing him to succeed.

That method wasn't in the manual, either, but she'd seen too many miraculous occurrences to discount the idea that dogs could sense a lot more than people gave them credit for. As her eyes stayed locked with Fremont's, she said a little prayer for his success.

"What are you doing?" Brian asked, wheeling back into the room. "Communing with his soul?"

"Something like that." Molly released the dog and got to her feet, stretching and yawning. "Oh, boy, am I beat."

"These are the best I can do," Brian said, holding two sleeveless shirts out to her. One was bright red, one black. "Put them both on so you won't be cold."

Molly accepted the shirts. "Yes, sir." The smile she forced was feeble. He was doing it again — proving he cared about her welfare and reminding her how little similar concern she'd known before. Why did he have to keep doing that? And why was it so hard to accept? After all, she'd have done the same for him.

The realization took her breath away. She sank back onto the couch. She would do the same for him. She had. And her behavior was based on more than mere concern for her fellow man. When she'd asked Brian to dinner, there had been more to the invitation than simple kindness. She had wanted him to come, to be with her, to share her house and all she had. It was the act of a would-be lover, not just a friend. Sharing and giving came naturally because Brian was already so much a part of living, of the enjoyment of her life, that to be without him meant something important was missing.

Molly hugged the shirts to her chest. They were clean, but nevertheless bore his unique masculine scent. She drank in the pleasant, earthy aroma. "Thank you."

"You're welcome." He turned to leave. "I'll use the bathroom off the master bedroom tonight. The one where you showered this morning is all yours."

"Do whatever's easier for you," she said quietly.

"The master bath doesn't have a bar for lifting myself, but I'll manage," he called back. "I have before."

She got up and hurried after him. "That's silly. I don't mind sharing a bathroom with you. I already took a shower and changed when I got home from work and —"

Brian wheeled around to block her path down the hall. "Go to bed, Molly. Leave me alone. I'm fine."

Still clasping his shirts to her chest, she stopped and stared at him. The tension between them was almost palpable. Although his expression reflected anger, there was a far more disturbing element to it.

Neither of them spoke. Molly wondered why her muscles seemed unwilling to let her retreat, yet left her equally unable to take another step closer to Brian. If he hadn't broken the spell and turned away, she suspected they might have remained as they were for a much longer time.

It wasn't until he'd entered his room and shut the door behind him that she finally went back to the living room. Undressing, she slipped both sleeveless shirts over her head. They didn't hang down quite as low as her teddy-bear shirt had, but they'd suffice. Draping her clean clothes over a chair, she headed for the bathroom.

A soft, scraping sound at Brian's door caught her attention. In the confusion, Fremont had been shut out. That wouldn't do. The dog was supposed to sleep with Brian to be available to attend to any needs he might have during the night. Barefoot, she padded down the hall. There was still a beam of light shining out under the door so she knocked.

"Just a minute," Brian called. Then, "All right."

Molly opened the door. "Fremont was left outside. It's best you keep him with you at all times."

"I know that." Brian's nostrils flared, his body coming alive at the sight of her. Her nipples were hardening beneath the shirts, and the larger armholes gave him a scant view of the gentle swell of the sides of her bare breasts. It wasn't much — less, actually, than would be glimpsed in a bathing suit. That didn't matter to Brian. What his eyes couldn't see, his imagination created.

Wide-eyed, Molly stared at him. Bedclothes covered only the lower half of his body, leaving his chest bare. When he lifted himself to adjust his position, muscles rippled beneath his smooth skin. The hair on his chest wasn't thick, but it was dark and curly, narrowing to a point as it descended to his waist. She'd always supposed that the rest of Brian's muscles were as well developed as his arms. Seeing for herself, she realized she'd underestimated his strength and the sheer masculine beauty of his body. Naturally, he'd be naked beneath the covers. Molly shivered.

"Well?" he demanded. "Was that all?"

"I . . . Yes." She slowly closed the door, leaving Fremont with his master. *Her* master was more like it, she mused, reveling in the rush of excitement that had not yet begun to diminish. She'd probably made a fool of her self, staring, but she couldn't make herself look away.

Mumbling incoherently, Molly went back to the dark living room. It was a darned good thing she hadn't followed through on her idea to try to seduce the poor man. If she had, she was sure she'd have failed miserably. One look at his naked chest had rendered her practically catatonic. Some seductress. If she remembered correctly, she hadn't even managed to smile at him.

With a weary sigh, she laid down on the couch, wrapped the blanket around her and closed her eyes. All she could see in the darkness behind her eyelids was Brian's naked body in bed, and that was not conducive to sleep. Now that she thought about it, his bedroom was more the way she'd imagined his whole house would be — warm and slightly cluttered and very masculine. It gave her a feeling of home she encountered rarely in other places. Of course, having Brian as the center of it all didn't hurt, either.

She sighed. Oh, well, even if she couldn't sleep, her fantasies were pleasant.

Commanding Fremont to go to the wall by the door and turn off the light, Brian laid back in bed. No woman in silk or satin had ever looked as good to him as Molly did in those stupid cotton shirts. He made a sound of disgust and shoved one of his pillows out of the way before closing his eyes.

They popped open again. Damn woman. Why did she affect him so? It was as if he'd known her forever, yet he supposed he didn't know her at all. She and Fremont had filled a void in his life that the dog alone was supposed to take care of.

Hearing the click of Fremont's nails on the floor as he returned from the successful completion of his task and laid down quietly beside the bed, Brian reached over the side. Fremont licked his hand.

"What're we going to do, old boy?" Brian asked.

A soft whine was the dog's reply.

"Yeah, I know. I miss her, too." Sighing, Brian petted the velvety fur. "But she's got a life of her own, and we don't fit into her plans. We both need to remember that."

He tried closing his eyes again. Once more, Molly's image floated through his mind, only this time, she was dressed in a satin teddy just like the one he'd described to her earlier.

Breathing unevenly, Brian made a decision. When he went to the mall to replace her ruined sleep shirt, he'd also get some other nice things for her. Sexy things. He began to smile. Molly, of course, would pitch a royal fit over it. Let her. If he accomplished nothing else to repay her for her kindnesses, at least maybe he could teach her to appreciate herself and not try to avoid attracting a man's attention.

His jaw clenched. A man like Keith, maybe, or some other young, good-looking hunk who could make her happy. The frustration level built within him till Brian wanted to shout at the unfairness of life. Instead, he reached down to help his lower extremities turn over, rolled onto his side, balled a pillow under his head and waited for sleep to overtake him.

It was a long time in coming.

By the time Brian arose the next morning, Molly was already up and about. His first clue was the aroma of coffee brewing. He got himself dressed and met her in the kitchen.

She held a steaming mug in her hand and was sipping from it. "Good morning."

"Good morning," he said. "I thought you hated getting up early."

"I did. It's still not my favorite time of day, but I figured if I had at least one cup of coffee by the time you joined me, I might not bite your head off."

"And . . . ?" Accepting the mug she placed on the table for him, he added cream and stirred. "Is it safe, yet?"

"I'm not sure. I still feel a bit like a hibernating bear who's been rudely awakened. Guess it's genetic."

"Maybe." Nodding, he took a swallow of coffee. "Speaking of sleeping reminds me of your shirt. Fremont and I are going shopping this morning. I'm making him use his allowance to buy you a replacement teddy bear."

The fact that Brian was still referring to Fremont as if he were a child rather than a dog struck her funny. "He gets what, fifty cents a week?"

"When he mows the lawn and picks up his toys," Brian quipped. "But he's been saving up."

"Oh, I see." She regarded the black Labrador as he sat expectantly beside Brian's chair. "Seriously. How's he been doing?"

"Surprisingly well," Brian said. Going to the back door, he opened it, gave the dog the okay and watched him bound happily into the yard. "I figured I'd put him through his paces in the mall while I shopped."

"If you wait till lunchtime, I can go with you."

Brian wanted to go alone. His plans for Molly's special gifts depended on it. "Tell you what. I'll give it a try this morning and if he causes too much trouble, we'll come back to FFI, get you and try again. Okay?"

She nodded. "I'm pleased you're feeling so independent." After a short pause, she added, "That is the idea, you know."

"I know." Ignoring the seriousness of her tone, he went to the refrigerator and peered inside. "Eggs? Toast? Bacon?"

"I'm not really hungry."

"We both have to eat," he insisted. "I'll make scrambled eggs again." With an apologetic grin, he looked over his shoulder at her. "I never did get to the store for dish soap. Before I go to the mall, I'll load the machine so you won't have to bother cleaning up by hand."

"It's no bother," Molly said. "I don't mind."

"But as you said, the idea is for me to become more independent." Her look of distress wasn't lost on him. "If you keep helping me out, I won't form a routine of my own that works without you, will I?"

"No. I suppose you won't." She'd thought he'd at least reiterate how much help she'd been and lament the fact she'd soon have to go. Apparently he wasn't going to miss her nearly as much as she was going to miss being with him. That figured. No one had ever found her indispensable. As a child, she'd felt as though she were invisible most of the time.

"Good. Then it's agreed," he said. "I'll cook and clean up the mess."

"That's the best offer I've had in a long time." Molly was working hard to appear lighthearted. She smiled as Fremont let himself in the back door and went straight to Brian for orders.

"Get the frying pan. There," Brian said, pointing to a cupboard.

The dog opened the door.

"Low," Brian told him, indicating a nearly floor-level shelf. As soon as Fremont's inquisitive nose touched the pan's handle, Brian said, "That's it. Get it. Hold. Bring it here."

With the handle of the heavy skillet in his mouth, Fremont managed to deliver it to Brian without dropping it.

"Good boy!" He fussed over the dog exuberantly. "What a good boy."

Grinning, Brian glanced over at Molly. "See? I told you he'd snapped out of whatever was bothering him. Isn't that great? I couldn't have reached that far down myself without really straining or maybe dumping the chair."

"I know." Her pride in Fremont swelled.

"It must have been that serious talk you had with him last night."

"Maybe so." Setting her half-empty coffee cup on the sink, Molly headed for the door to the hall. "While you're doing that, I'll go braid my hair."

He looked up. "I could do it for you."

"I don't think that's such a good idea, do you?" The tremor in her voice added seriousness to the question as she paused at the door.

"No," he said, equally as solemn. "I *don't* think it's a very good idea. I'm sorry I didn't get you the mirrors you needed."

"It doesn't matter. I won't be here much longer."

"I'm sorry about that, too."

She noted the depth of feeling in his voice, the fondness and friendship in his eyes. He was going to miss her at least a little.

"Me, too," Molly confessed. "But it's for the best."

"Yes, I know." Seated next to the stove, he watched her turn away and leave the room.

Fremont's cold nose nudged his hand and he absently patted the dog's head. Brian knew he had to let Molly go, he'd always known, so why was it getting harder and harder to accept? Why was he torturing himself by imagining she wanted to stay? And then what? A young woman in her prime didn't belong with someone like him.

He thought of Albert and Lillian. They seemed happy, yet how long could something like that last? In that respect, Molly had probably been right. It was a mistake to think like an able bodied man when you weren't. Illusions were for children, and marital bliss was for other people. That much was certain.

Could he and Molly remain friends, he wondered, or would her interest wane as soon as Fremont had satisfactorily proved his reliability? Of that, Brian wasn't sure. He'd like to think Molly was his friend the same way Joyce and Sam were, but only time would tell him if that was true.

Scrambling the eggs and dumping them into the hot pan, he passed the empty cardboard carton to Fremont to put into the trash. The dog looked puzzled while he followed Brian's directions, but did as he was told and received the usual flowery praise. Tail wagging, he returned to sit beside his master.

"I made enough eggs for you, too," Brian told the attentive dog. "Since you helped so much, I figured you deserved a treat."

"It does smell good," Molly said, reentering the kitchen. "I hope you cooked enough to feed all three of us."

"Just like the three musketeers," Brian quipped. "Have a seat D'Artagnan, it's almost ready."

"I'll get the plates and forks," Molly said. "Dog lips on my silverware is not a favorite flavor of mine."

"I never pictured you as prejudiced."

"Hygienic is more like it," she explained. "I don't mind most things, but I do like clean eating utensils."

"Fremont would share with you," Brian reminded her.

Molly laughed. "I know. He has. Until you're absolutely sure of him, I suggest you don't put a hamburger on a low table or leave your lunch on the seat of the car beside him and walk away." She realized instantly what she'd inadvertently said. The look on Brian's face told her he, too, had caught the slip.

"I promise I won't walk anywhere," he said, bringing the hot pan to the table by resting it on a pad on his lap.

"It was a figure of speech," she said defensively.

"But apropos. It doesn't pay to forget what I am."

That did it. Molly had spent a nearly sleepless night and awakened already on edge, and now Brian was playing the martyr. Again. Some of that attitude was inevitable, but he seemed to dredge it up handily every time she said or did something that displeased him. She was tired of walking on eggs. It was time somebody told him to knock off the self-denigration. It was time she told him.

"What you are is a stubborn, obstinate man who's learned to enjoy pitying himself," she said, her hands on her hips. "Get off it, Forrester. Grow up."

Her irate outburst took Brian by surprise. The worst part was, her words hit home. "Damn." He slammed the pan down on the table. "Damn it. You're right."

Molly stared at him, her eyes wide and expressive. "I know I am. What I don't understand is how come you accepted my conclusions so easily."

"Probably because I've known the truth for some time now. It just seemed wrong, somehow, to release the hurt, to let go of the anger. Does that make sense?"

"No. But you have to remember, I've never been handicapped. I'm not the one to ask."

"I saw a shrink while I was in the hospital.

He said I was fine. You, obviously, know me better than he did."

"I'm glad." And she truly was. Her heart told her that Brian wasn't sick in the way a lot of psychiatric patients were and that was probably why the hospital psychiatrist had passed him off as well. The problem was that Brian was also not fully healed. It was the unresolved conflicts within him that were keeping him off balance. The anger was merely its outward manifestation. Molly knew instinctively that once he was able to forgive himself for being injured in the first place, he'd feel much better.

She smiled at him and passed him a fork. "Does that mean I can bill you for services rendered?"

Reaching out before she could withdraw her hand, Brian grasped and held it. "Since the first day I met you, I've known you were going to be my salvation, Molly. There isn't enough money in the whole universe to pay you adequately for that."

Easing away gently, she reclaimed her hand and sat down opposite him. "In that case, don't try. Let's just be friends and count ourselves lucky to have met."

"I'd like that," he said. "It's all I'd hoped for."

She held out her empty plate as she nodded

toward the pan of eggs. "Then feed me, old buddy, before I starve."

On the floor beside Brian, Fremont woofed in agreement.

Brian glanced down. "So go get your dish, too," he said. "I'm not the pizza man. I don't deliver."

Molly was laughing by the time the dog had figured out how to grab the slippery, conical dish. He ended up dropping it and pushing it along the floor with his nose.

"Whatever works, that's what I say," Brian commented as he leaned down to ladle egg into the dog's dish.

"That's good advice," Molly said, "in all areas of life."

"From psychiatrist to philosopher in minutes," Brian announced. "Here she is, ladies and gentlemen . . . and dogs, the eighth wonder of the world, Ms. Molly Evans."

"I also managed to braid my own hair this morning." She turned so he could see. "Is it fairly neat?"

"Good enough for a ride in my Austin. By the time you get to work, who'll know the difference?"

She was smiling at the thought. "Can I keep the goggles? I mean, after my van is fixed." Molly busied herself eating so she wouldn't have to look at Brian when she asked.

"Of course. I told you they were a gift."

"I know. I thought maybe you were kidding."

"If I say something is for you, it's for you," he insisted. "I don't kid about stuff like that."

"Good," she said. "I wanted a memento."

"Did you?" His heart swelled with love for her. That she'd wanted something by which to remember him touched him deeply. "Is there anything else I can give you? Just ask."

Molly did well not to choke on her breakfast. There was no doubt in her mind that Brian Forrester was capable of giving her the love she yearned for. Conversely, he was also capable of rejecting her. Past experience had not provided her with the emotional tools she thought she needed in order to please him. When he laughed at her feeble attempts at seduction — and she knew he would — it would kill her. Oh, no. What she wanted was far too unpredictable to ever ask for.

She concentrated on her plate and quickly finished eating. It had occurred to her, part way through the interminable night, that her idea of offering to make love to Brian wasn't altogether unselfish. Nor was it wise. All they'd really done so far was share a few kisses and yet, even the thought of his touch made her tingle all over and tied enormous, throbbing knots in her abdomen. What could she hope to salvage of her emotions if she encouraged a deeper intimacy? As it was, she was branded for life.

Molly looked up. Brian had finished eating and seemed to be waiting for her to reply. "There's nothing I want that I don't have, but thanks for asking," she said. "Do you want to drive me to work again, or shall I phone Keith?"

Brian's jaw stiffened. "I told you. You don't need him. I'll take care of you." Pushing off, he left her alone in the kitchen.

"I know you would," Molly said quietly so he couldn't overhear. "The trouble is, I can't let you. I just can't."

Chapter Twelve

By the time Brian had dropped Molly at work, cleaned up the kitchen and left for the mall with Fremont, he'd worked out how he was going to get away with giving her the gifts he wanted her to have, without overstepping the bounds of propriety. Molly might be a modern, self-assured woman, but some of her ideas were still pretty Victorian. He knew she'd never accept lingerie from him no matter how desperately she wanted it or how much he wanted to give it to her. Therefore, he'd use an acceptable surrogate. Fremont.

Two ribbon-bedecked packages were waiting on the couch for her when Brian brought her home that evening. He saw from her expression that she was about to refuse them.

"A new teddy bear shirt," he quickly explained. "I owed it to you, remember?"

"Oh, sure. I'd forgotten." One eyebrow cocked. "And the other box? Did you get two bears?"

Brian shrugged. "I don't know. That one's not from me."

Both eyebrows arched. "Then who?"

Giving Fremont a hand signal, Brian sent him to the boxes. They'd rehearsed often enough so that he thought the dog had his role memorized. Still, there was always the element of chance when you were dealing with an animal.

As planned, Fremont picked up the smaller, lighter box. Bearing it proudly to Molly, he sat at her feet and held it.

Her natural instinct was to refuse, yet to do so would be contrary to the dog's training. The last thing Fremont needed at this stage of his development was more confusing human reactions.

She bent down and took the box. "Thank you, Fremont."

Tail wagging, he released Molly's gift and went quickly back to Brian's side.

"Way to go, boy," Brian whispered, his nervousness mounting. He wasn't sure why it was so important to him to have Molly accept the lingerie, but it was. Monumentally important. Not that he made a practice of giving such intimate gifts to women. He didn't. The last time he'd purchased something like the silk teddy, he'd intended it for Pam as a honeymoon surprise. After the accident, he'd found the unopened box and passed it on to Joyce with apologies. Sam, however, had assured him he hadn't minded at all when his wife had worn the lovely garment.

A warm flush stole up Brian's neck to redden his face. Molly hadn't even opened the box yet, and already he was blushing. And aroused. Damn it. Lifting the remaining box, he laid it across his lap to help hide his true feelings.

"You're telling me this is from Fremont?" Molly asked, trying not to smile.

"Guess so."

"And I suppose he also picked it out himself."

"Uh-huh." Brian chanced a slight smile and waited for her similar response. He wasn't disappointed.

"It's a rawhide chew, I'll bet."

"Um, I kind of doubt it. We didn't go into any pet-supply stores."

"Oh?" Molly seated herself on the couch, facing him, and began to toy with the ribbon on the box. "Just where did you go then?"

"The usual. Department stores. Specialty shops. Finding a teddy bear shirt was hard. I never did manage to match yours exactly." Coming closer, he handed her the box he held, then backed off.

"You remembered what my bear looked like? I'm surprised."

Remembered? Brian could replay the scenes of her in the shapeless shirt like a well-loved classic movie. It was Molly he focused on. The bear was there, but incidental.

"Which one should I open first?" she asked.

"Mine." He wanted her to accept the more customary offering before she had a chance to refuse the sexy teddy. That way, he'd at least have given her something.

Shuffling the boxes, she pulled on the gold ribbon circling Brian's gift. It fell away. Molly laid aside the box lid, pushed back the tissue paper and gazed upon the white shirt. It was folded so that the picture on the front showed. In it, two smiling bears held hands. Their images were surrounded by hearts, stars, butterflies and flowers. Below the picture were the words: Best Friends.

Molly's vision blurred. "Oh, Brian. It's perfect."

He let his breath out in a whoosh. "You like it?"

"Of course, I do." She lifted the shirt, looked at it a moment, then hugged it to her. "I love it. Thank you."

"I wanted you to remember me," he said, keeping his distance for both their sakes.

A tear escaped and she swiped at it. "You know I will."

Brian's voice was too loud, his tone overly hearty when he said, "So. Open the one from Fremont."

Silently, Molly laid aside his gift and concentrated on the smaller box. Whatever it contained, it was obvious Brian didn't want to take credit for giving it to her. It was also evident that he wanted her to know he was behind its selection. When the tissue fell back, it was clear to Molly why he'd handled it in that way.

She fingered the delicate, peach-colored silk trimmed with ecru lace, then looked over at him. "Brian, I —"

"Please. Don't say no. I realize it's totally inappropriate, but it really means a lot to me. You're a beautiful woman. You deserve beautiful things."

The sincerity in his demeanor, his expression, was unmistakable. To refuse the gift would be the same to Brian as she'd imagined his physical rejection of her would feel. Hurtful. There was only one way she could accept without compromising her personal ideals and she quickly took it.

Smiling pleasantly, she turned her attention to Fremont. "Thank you, darling. It's just what I wanted." Laying aside both boxes, she dropped to one knee in front of Brian and the dog, took the Lab's head in her hands and placed a kiss on his forehead.

"I helped pick it out," Brian offered.

"Did you? How sweet. I guess that's how

he managed to tell the salesgirl my size."

"He sort of held out his paws. Like this." Brian demonstrated.

"So clever." Molly kissed Fremont again.

"Hey! I loaned him the money."

"I thought you said he had to use his allowance."

"He was short. Now he's in debt to me for the next couple of years."

"Poor Fremont." Giving the dog a hug, Molly got to her feet. "Only two years old and already tangled up with a loan shark."

The smile on Molly's face was a bit sad, Brian noted, but she was doing her best to be funny as she played the silly game of pretend they'd enjoyed so much in the past. That was good enough for him. Thinking about reality and his future was the last thing he wanted to do anyway. While Molly was kidding around, they could both forget their inevitable parting.

He grinned. "I'll be gentle if he misses a payment."

"Good." Molly piled the boxes and gifts in the corner of the couch. "So . . . What shall we have for dinner? If you're broke now, thanks to Fremont's extravagances, I'll spring for a pizza."

"I have a few bucks left. Save your money. You need it."

"Are you still worrying about my wages?"

"A little, I guess. Friends are like that."

Molly nodded. "Speaking of megabucks, how's my van coming along? Is it going to cost me a bundle or what?"

"Or what. Sam is getting the parts wholesale."

She winced. "Would you like to spell it out for me? I need to plan ahead if it's going to be a big expense."

"Five dollars, max," Brian told her.

"What? That's ridiculous!"

"Okay. Four."

Getting to her feet, Molly paced away from him. "Don't be silly. Tell me the truth. What's it going to cost?"

He lowered his voice. "Nothing, Molly." When she opened her mouth to protest, he shushed her with a wave of his hand. "Don't you know what you and Sam did for me when you showed me I could still function as a mechanic?"

Molly waited, listening.

"You proved to me that at least part of me was still worth something. Even if I don't choose to work on engines all the time, I can if I want to. That's the kicker. I *can*."

"Of course, you can. I knew you could."

"You still don't get it, do you?" Brian pressed. "*You* may have known, but no way in hell was *I* going to believe you until I saw for myself. I had to prove it could be done by doing it." The volume of his voice dropped. "And it was terrifying."

"Because you hadn't considered it before?" Molly asked.

"No. Because if I failed, then I would have proved to myself what I'd only suspected up till then." Moving closer, he took her hand. "Don't you see? If I hadn't been able to do the work after I'd tried to, all my hope would have died then and there."

She gripped his warm, strong fingers. "I thought you were convinced you'd fail from the start. That's what you said."

"For self-defense, Molly. It was easier to claim inability and rest on that than to voice the hope that I might be able to go back to work. Failure was a given. Success was the dream."

"And now?"

He smiled fondly up at her. "You and Fremont have handed me back my life. Your van is the symbol of that to me. I'd never intended to charge you for the repairs when I figured Sam and the boys would be doing them. Now that it's me, that goes double. A man can't charge for a miracle. It's sacrilege."

There was nothing to do but agree, accept his favor and hope to someday pay it back by helping someone else on Brian's behalf. She nodded. "All right. How soon will the repairs be done?"

The parts were in the trunk of his Austin, but Brian hadn't installed them, yet. He'd had the time that afternoon, it was just that he was afraid Molly's stay might be shortened if he finished with her van too soon. Feeling guilty, he decided it was time to get on with it. Get it over with.

"I'll need you to help a little, turn on the ignition and such. I thought maybe tomorrow, since it's Saturday. It won't take long."

"Sure. I'll be glad to help you." She smiled. "I suppose Fremont can't be expected to manipulate keys."

"Not yet," Brian said. "But I'm working on it."

"I almost strangled trying not to laugh the first time I saw him in his driving goggles." Molly pulled hers from her purse and put them on. "What do you say we go cruising and stop for a pizza on the way home? It's a nice evening for a drive."

"You don't have to wear those," he told her. "Your sunglasses are fine." Commanding Fremont to the back door and letting him out, he returned. "I've locked the door so he can't get back in and chew up your new teddy bears. Shall we go?"

"Fremont can come."

"Not this time," Brian said flatly. "Not for what may be our last ride."

"How do you know it will be?" Molly's eyes lowered, and she studied the toes of her tennis shoes.

"I'm psychic." Sensing her tense reaction to his humorless reply, he relented. "What I mean is, I'm practical. Fremont is fine. As soon as you have wheels, I suspect you're planning to leave. Am I right?"

"Yes." She couldn't look at him, couldn't think of anything funny or lighthearted to say. Stripping off the goggles, she tossed them onto the couch with the gifts Brian had bought her and put on her dark glasses. They were best. They covered the pain she knew had to be reflected in her eyes.

Molly didn't normally drink beer, but Brian had ordered a pitcher of the stuff along with their pizza and her thirst convinced her the taste wasn't bad combined with adequate amounts of pepperoni and cheese. Besides, the headache she'd been fighting all day seemed to be lessening in direct proportion to her consumption of beer.

"Aren't you going to join me?" she asked, raising her mug.

"No more for me. I'm driving."

"We shouldn't waste it."

Brian refilled her mug and leaned on the table, watching her. Molly was a funny person; overly sentimental and outgoing about many things, yet totally guarded with regard to her private life. Hell, he didn't even know if she drank, as a rule. From her reactions to the beer, he doubted it.

"I remember Sam and me getting sloshed once when we were young," he remarked. "It was no fun. If I were you, I'd take it easy on that stuff if you're not used to it."

She froze, the mug held in her hand, her eyes widening. "I — I don't usually drink at all." Lowering the frosty mug slowly, she pushed it aside and traced a ring of water on the tabletop with one finger. "It's easy to get carried away, isn't it? I'd never realized that before."

Brian studied her. She seemed to be wrestling with an unspoken dilemma. He placed his hand over hers. "Want to tell me about it?"

"It was a long time ago."

"And the alcoholic was close to you?"

Asking him how he knew, her gaze raised to his. "Yes. My father."

Brian closed his fingers around hers. "It's past. Let it go."

She shook her head. "I wish I could. He

213

was such a good man when he was sober and such a monster when he wasn't. My mother was deathly afraid of him."

"But you weren't?"

Molly's laugh was humorless. "I pretended not to be. It was the best way to handle him."

So that was why she trembled when anyone raised his voice to her. He doubted she was aware the effect was so evident. "What finally happened?"

"They got a divorce. It was ugly. Everyone expected me to take sides the way my sister and brother did. I refused, so they *all* disowned me. Except Mom. She moved to Florida. I hear from her once in a while." Molly felt a bit dizzy, and queasiness began to flutter her stomach.

"And that's why you decided marriage was stupid? One example is hardly a fair test."

Molly snorted a chuckle. "One? Try six. My whole family is a walking ad for divorce lawyers. Nobody's stayed married. My sister's on her third husband, and my brother is supporting two wives and three children."

Brian didn't know what else to say. It was obvious her life had been a hard one. And a lonely one.

"How old were you when your parents divorced?"

"Eighteen. But it all started way before that.

Mother was forever moving out and leaving the three of us to deal with Dad. My sister had to look after me from the time I was nine or ten. She did the best she could, but I really hated it. I suppose she did, too. Then our mother would come back and the cycle would repeat. That's why, when I was seventeen, I moved out and went to work at the clinic."

"Whoa. Back up a little. You haven't always worked with dogs?" His interest was piqued. It amazed him that there was so much he didn't know about Molly. He'd told her almost all there was to know about him and his past.

"No." She began to smile wistfully. "I was a physical therapist's assistant for a while. It was fascinating work."

"And FFI? How did you get started there?"

"A patient at the clinic had an assistance dog. I met him, raised one puppy for the group, then fell into training as if I'd been born to do it."

"Maybe you were."

Sighing, she drew her hand out from under his. "Maybe. I suppose it's easier to believe in total predestination if you've been happy all your life. I do think, though, that I was meant to help people through FFI."

"That was one of the things about you that impressed me from the start," Brian told her. "You seemed so alive, so enthusiastic about what you were doing. It was a joy to watch."

"Thank you." Sliding to the end of the bench, she got to her feet. "Now I think we'd better be going, don't you?" Another wave of dizziness swept over her and she steadied herself by grabbing the edge of the table. "Oh, dear."

"Here." Brian rolled up behind her, took her by the waist and guided her into his lap. "I'll give you a ride to the car."

She slipped one arm around his neck. "Like Albert and Lillian at the graduation party?"

Brian started for the door. "I guess so. I didn't stay long enough to see him do it, but he once told me he liked to carry her on his lap."

As they approached the pizza parlor's exit, Molly reached out with her foot and gave the door a hard push. In two strokes of Brian's arms, they were outside. The temperature had dropped with the setting of the sun. Shivering, she cuddled closer and lowered her head to his shoulder.

He stopped by the Austin, set the chair's brake and closed his arms around her. Hold her, that's all he'd do. Just hold her. Make memories. And ache for her. Ache until he thought he'd die from the wanting, the needing — the love he was no longer fool enough to deny.

Molly's alcohol consumption hadn't been so great that she couldn't notice his evident arousal. Turning slightly, she pressed herself even closer, wanting to feel every inch of him one last time.

"Don't." His hands spanned her ribs. "I can't take it if you move much more."

She lifted her head to study his face. "Am I too heavy?"

"In a manner of speaking."

"I'll get up." Reaching out, she held on to the car door and pulled herself to her feet. Brian leaned forward, his hands at her waist. When she was standing, he didn't release her.

"I'm not dizzy anymore."

"Don't go."

She pivoted and put her hands over his. Primitive feelings urged her to glance at his lap.

"Yeah," he said cynically "That part seems to work."

Swallowing, Molly nodded. "Aren't you glad?"

"Sure. Now all I have to do is find some woman who can stand to be around the rest of me and who won't laugh her head off if I can't perform."

"I think you're selling women short, Brian. We're not all like Pam."

"And all men are not like your father." He

released her. "Get in the car. I'll take you home."

"To your house?" She asked the question in a whisper, afraid he intended to deliver her to her own doorstep.

"For tonight," he said. "Tomorrow we'll finish your van and you can leave."

"I suppose that would be best."

"Best? Hah! Lady, it's damn near imperative."

Without even bidding Molly a polite good-night, Brian left her in the living room, got Fremont and took him with him to his room, shutting the door behind them.

Molly sank dejectedly onto the couch. Bummer. The whole situation was a bummer. The only one who seemed the least bit happy was Fremont, and even he had grown subdued when he'd encountered the tension that had hung over her and Brian since dinner.

She reached out to stretch and her left hand touched the edges of the gift boxes. Dear, sweet man. It must have been really embarrassing for him to shop for such apparel, yet he'd done it. For her. It would be a shame if the garments didn't fit, because she intended to wear them — both of them — to remember him by.

Molly started for the bathroom. It had been

a long, wearying day. First she'd shower and wash her hair. Then she'd try on Brian's gifts. If either of them were the wrong size, he'd have tomorrow to make an exchange. Love swelled and pulsed within her. How could she go away? How could she bear to leave him?

She glanced down the hall on her way to the bath room. Brian's door was closed, the light off. Her heart lurched. He lay behind that door, alone and convinced he'd never be able to satisfy a woman. For a virile man like Brian, that must be the worst fate imaginable. She knew he was wrong. It only remained to be proven.

Heart pounding, Molly dashed into the bathroom and shut the door. Leaning on it, she tried to catch her breath. To desert him, leave him, still feeling as though he was a failure would be a terrible crime. She couldn't. Not when she knew she could help him see the truth.

Turning on the shower, she unplaited her hair while she waited for the water to heat up. By the time she stepped under the stinging spray, she'd decided what to do. He might not like it, but Brian Forrester was going to get a late-night visit from his fairy godmother. She just hoped his magical wish was the same as hers.

Chapter Thirteen

Before her hair was dry, Molly was sure she must have changed her mind, back and forth, at least a hundred times. The silk teddy was even lovelier as it clung to her body. Although her original plan had been to boldly approach Brian wearing nothing else, she found that actually doing it was harder than simply imagining it. In the end, she'd slipped the teddy-bear sleep shirt over the top like a robe.

Standing in the darkened hall, she rehearsed what she would do and say. Trying to picture herself acting like a slinky siren and purring like a cat only made her feel silly. Silly enough to call the whole thing off. The idea was pure foolishness anyway. Just because a man had a simple physical reaction to a woman didn't mean he wanted to make love to her, did it? Or did it?

And so what if he did? What made her think she was the right one to prove his manhood to him? On the contrary, she was probably the *worst* choice. Brian needed a practiced lover who knew how to move, how to please a man, how to substitute her own skills for whatever lack he might have.

Molly gritted her teeth and turned away, went three paces, then stopped. She wanted to open his door. Every inch of her cried out to be held in his arms, to taste his kisses again, to lay beside him and run her fingers up and down his full length to show him there was no part of him she couldn't love.

An enormous fist closed inside her, pulling her in, in, until she wanted to shout Brian's name and run to him. She found herself again standing before the closed door. She reached for the knob, then paused.

Coward! Worthless woman! She couldn't do it. It was like being poised at the edge of the highest diving board at the municipal swimming pool, your toes hanging over the edge, knowing one small act would send you hurtling into the water, yet not being able to take that last, fateful step.

Molly didn't know why her hesitation surprised her. It shouldn't. She'd been there before. Not with Brian, of course, and not dressed in a sexy teddy, but she had passed up other opportunities to become intimate. For her the act of love went hand in hand with marriage. Fashionable or not, that was her view. To make love was to trust in a person, to look toward the future together. Molly Evans had never been able to do that.

She sighed as she turned away. Brian would never have to know she'd been there or how close she'd come to opening the door, both to his room and to her heart.

She took one step down the hall, then another. A slight sound came to her in the near darkness. Stopping, she reached for the light switch, flipped it on and listened. Fremont's nails were clicking on the floor in Brian's room. The doorknob began to turn.

"Molly!" Brian called out. "Molly!"

Panic filled his voice as if he were hurt or in distress. All thought of hesitation fled from Molly's mind. Pushing the door the rest of the way open, she did the only thing her love for him would allow — she ran to him and fell into his waiting arms.

"What is it, darling? Are you in pain?"

Brian held her as if the world were about to end and they had but seconds left together. "Oh, God, Molly. I was dreaming. I thought you were gone."

"I'm here." She rained kisses over his neck and shoulder. "It's all right. I'm here."

Regaining some control over his irregular breathing, Brian loosened his hold on her as he noticed the light from the hall coming through the half-open door. "How did you know I wanted you? Were you still up?"

"Yes. Fremont let me in."

"He went to fetch you?" Brian saw no sign of his dog.

"In a way." Stroking his cheek, Molly gazed down at him. "I was standing right outside in the hall."

His brow furrowed. "Why?"

"Because I was too much of a coward to come in."

Brian slid his hand to her waist, traced the curve of her hip and finally brought his palm to rest on her thigh. "You were coming to me?" He hardly dared hope he was right. Ever since their enlightening conversation over dinner, he'd been thinking about Molly and marriage, never daring to dream she'd consider accepting him even if he proposed. And now here she was, the answer to all his prayers.

"I was." Her voice was little more than a whisper.

His hand moved higher, caressing, loving every inch of her. When he encountered the lace edge of the teddy under the sleep shirt, he stopped, his eyes pleading with her to let him see all the treasures she had hidden from his gaze.

Understanding, Molly stood, crossed her arms and lifted the teddy bears over her head. She heard Brian's sharp intake of breath. The look on his face was illuminated by the light from the hall, and she could swear there was moisture in his eyes.

"It's all right?" she asked, turning slowly in a full circle.

"Beautiful." He reached for her.

The catch in his voice was the most erotic sound she'd ever heard. Opening her arms, she fell across his chest, her hair sweeping down to cover her own tears of joy. This was right. No matter what society or anyone else said, being with Brian was right, meant to be, just like her mission to help the handicapped by training special dogs.

He raised her face with his hands, drew her closer and kissed her, the draught long and sustaining. There were no other women in the world for him, save Molly, nor would there ever be. He could almost be grateful for his accident, because it was what had brought her into his life. Thank God he was free to make her his own!

Molly returned his kisses with a fervor she hadn't suspected she possessed, her hands brushing over his chest and shoulders and down to where the bedclothes lay.

"Wait." Taking her shoulders, he set her away, then threw back the covers that separated them and welcomed her back into his embrace. When she hid her face in the crook of his shoulder, he placed a light kiss on her hair.

"Are you embarrassed?"

"A little."

"Stretch out. Lay by me. We'll go slowly."

It was all Brian could do to keep his promise. If he'd been able to roll over easily, he'd have had her pinned to the bed by now. In Molly's case, it was just as well he'd be forced by his physical limitations to take his time. The last thing he wanted to do was frighten her when she'd only just begun to trust him.

Taking her hand from where it rested on his chest, he kissed her fingertips, then placed them on his stomach. "You gave me back my life, Molly. I'm a man again because of you." He guided her lower, inch by inch. "I want you to touch me." His voice broke. "Please . . . ?"

She snuggled closer and draped one leg over his, her thigh telling her of the wonders her fingers would soon caress. How she yearned to belong to Brian, to please him until no doubt remained to ever again make him question his virility.

Slowly, tentatively, she stroked his abdomen, then passed her hand around his waist and down over his hip. The change from normal muscle tension to that of his lower extremities was evident.

"Can you feel this?" she asked, expertly kneading the twitching muscles of his thigh

225

the way she'd been trained to as a physical therapist.

"No."

Her hand moved to the inside of his leg. "Here?"

"No." Barely breathing, Brian waited. Looking down he could see every move she was making. If only he could feel her touch.

Molly was trembling as she brought her hand up to caress him as he'd wanted. This time, she didn't have to ask. His sharp intake of breath told her he could, indeed, tell what she was doing.

"Oh, God, Molly!" He threw back his head, ecstasy cloaking his features, and moaned.

Encouraged, she lifted herself and scattered kisses across his shoulder and neck.

All at once, strong hands gripped her arm. "Stop. Please."

She did. Brian was breathing rapidly, but then so was she. Never had she imagined making love could be so glorious, so all encompassing. The only thing she didn't quite understand was why he'd stopped her when they were both so eager.

"Did I hurt you?"

Lifting her to lie partially on top of him, he shook his head. "No. Not hurt. Didn't you feel what was about to happen?"

Molly let her hair hang down to hide her

face from him and shook her head. "No. That is, I don't know." She tried to pull away, but he held her fast. "Please don't be disappointed. You're fine. The problem is mine."

At that, Brian relaxed a little, pulled her closer and laughed softly. "The 'problem' is mine and has been since the first time I was fool enough to kiss you, Molly. And now that my wildest fantasies have been realized and I have you in my bed, it occurs to me I have an even worse problem."

Handicapped or not, the responsibility was his and he wasn't about to shirk it. If by his carelessness Molly be came pregnant . . .

The thought sang along his taut nerves and settled in his soul. This was no game they were playing. It was for real. Forever.

His jaw clenched. And if he failed her, what then? A sweet girl like Molly wouldn't throw him over for it, but she should if he couldn't be a proper husband to her. The idea of maybe losing her over an inability to perform took a lot of the fire out of him.

Raising on one elbow, Molly gazed into his eyes. Perhaps he wasn't too discouraged with her clumsy attempts to continue. "If it's confidence you need, I'm sure you'll do fine."

"Confidence I have. It's proper protection for you I don't have," he said, coloring. "I don't suppose you brought any along when you decided to pay me this visit." Not ready to face the chance of failure straight on, he almost hoped she hadn't.

"No." Truthfully, she'd not even thought of birth control. That showed how worldly *she* was. "I didn't exactly plan ahead."

Enfolding her in a bone-crushing embrace, Brian held her close. "That's all right. We've waited all our lives. We can wait one more night." He chuckled, still breathless, but very relieved. "At least, I think we can."

"No!" Twisting away, Molly sat up. "We can't wait. I'll be gone. It has to be tonight!" Lord, she couldn't believe she'd said that! It sounded like an order for the poor man to make love to her. "I — I don't have — I mean, I'm healthy, if that's what's worrying you. I've never . . ." She turned away.

Brian took her hand. "Look at me, Molly." When she finally did, he spoke seriously. "There'll be other nights for us. I don't want you to ever leave. I love you."

"Don't say that!"

"Why shouldn't I? There are lots of things I don't understand about you, honey, but one thing I am sure of. You would never have come to my bed like this if you didn't feel the same way about me." Waiting, he saw fear light her eyes.

"I don't love you," she lied.

"I don't believe you." Brian refused to let himself believe her. If it wasn't love that had brought her to him in the night, then what had? What, indeed? The options were endless. Had he fallen madly in love and been blinded to other possibilities? Molly was a natural-born giver. What was she trying to give him? By God, she'd better be ready to spell it out.

His grip on her fingers tightened before he let her go. "Then why? Curiosity? Pity? What?"

The anger in his voice didn't frighten her anymore. If anything, it gave her hope that he'd been kidding himself about being in love with her. If that were true, it would make her departure much less traumatic — for him, anyway.

Molly gently touched his bare shoulder. The warm, smooth skin quivered beneath her fingers. "You said you were worried you couldn't please a woman. I just thought . . ."

Brian shook her off. "You thought you'd provide a nice little ego boost?" he shouted. "Give the poor cripple something to remember you by?"

"Brian, don't."

"What a joke on me. Here I thought all along that a beautiful, sensitive woman had gone and fallen in love with me in spite of my legs."

"Any woman could," Molly offered, still hoping to make him understand while not sure she, herself, did.

"*Any* woman? That's a laugh."

Molly sprang to her feet and stood beside the bed, her hands on her hips, mindless of the revealing teddy. "Why? Because somebody like me, whose love life is zip, didn't fall head over heels for you? What did you do, figure I was desperate?"

Calming himself with great effort, Brian raised on his elbows and stared at her. "No. Not desperate. Blind. My legs may not work, but *your* paralysis is worse. It's in your heart, and it's made you fear the very thing that can cure you . . . love."

"That's a lie."

"Prove it. Admit you love me, too."

She backed toward the door. "I don't have to prove anything to you. I won't." Before her tears got the better of her, she ducked out into the hall and ran.

Exhausted, Brian sank back on the pillows. In spite of her vehement denial, he'd be willing to bet every cent he had that Molly did love him. She was too noble to have behaved as she had if it wasn't for love. And he'd received her gift of herself poorly. Caution was logical, sure, but there had been times in his past when he'd overlooked logic in the throes of passion.

Brian sighed. In truth, he'd been too scared to think clearly, and he'd taken his anger at himself out on her. If she weren't so innocent about men, she'd have realized that no normal man could call a halt so easily in the middle of lovemaking if there weren't something else stopping him.

He lifted his legs off the edge of the bed and sat up. He didn't care if it took him all night, he'd make Molly understand. She deserved to see all the way into his heart so she would know there was no deceit hiding there, waiting to hurt her.

His slacks lay draped across his chair with his other clothes. Pulling the chair closer, he took the time to at least don his pants. In Molly's agitated state, he wasn't going to chase after her stark naked, even if he wanted to.

Fremont joined him, looking confused. Brian pointed to the dog's usual spot on the floor beside the bed. "You lay there. Stay." Fremont obeyed as Brian transferred to his wheelchair. A shirt and shoes weren't necessary. All he wanted to do was go to Molly and talk. That was all. Just talk. If she'd listen.

The dog's tail thumped and he started to get up to follow Brian.

"No, Fremont. Don't. Stay here. I'll convince her to stay for both our sakes." Brian pushed off toward the open door. "She has to. We'll both be lost without our Molly."

Fremont woofed softly.

"Yeah. I'll give her your love, too," Brian said. "In the meantime, don't wreck the place, okay?" Swinging around at the door, he pulled it closed behind him. Whatever happened between him and Molly in the living room, he didn't need a cold, wet dog's nose poking in where it wasn't wanted.

Nervous, Brian smiled. Oh, Molly, he thought, you have to marry me! Don't you see how perfect we are for each other? He paused, rehearsing different ways to propose. None of them sounded the way he wanted them to. None were convincing enough to suit him.

Don't panic, he told himself. Just go to her. Say what's in your heart. Be yourself and trust that the same Power which brought you together in the first place will finish the job. He shot a wordless prayer heavenward.

Cruising into the living room, he looked toward the couch, expecting to see Molly sitting or lying there. His smile faded. Her blanket was folded neatly at one end and her pillow still rested at the other, but something was definitely amiss.

Brian glanced around the room. Nothing else remained to indicate Molly Evans had been there. Her purse, shoes and clothes were gone.

Nostrils flaring, Brian hurried into the kitchen. No sign of her. He'd passed by the extra bedroom, so he knew she wasn't in there, either.

"Face it, Forrester," he muttered. "She's gone." Rolling to the front door, he opened it and saw both Molly's van and his car in the driveway. Of course, she wouldn't take his car, and he'd foolishly seen to it that she couldn't escape in her van. Therefore, she must have left on foot. Walking. In the middle of the night along an unlighted, winding road. Oh, God! What had he done?

Brian snatched up his keys off the table. He had to find her. Whether she ever accepted his love or not, he had to make sure she was safe.

In his haste, he almost upset the chair. Lifting himself into the Austin, he shoved the wheelchair away and slammed the car door. If he didn't locate Molly along the road, the chair would do him no good anyway and he'd waste precious seconds folding and loading it.

No. The sports car would be his legs for this particular emergency. Once he was certain Molly had arrived home safely, then he'd worry about himself. For the present, she was all that mattered.

Jamming the car into gear, he roared out of the driveway. *Oh, Molly, please be safe. Dear Lord, please let her be safe.* If there were such things as guardian angels, he prayed that Molly's was on the job. Fog was rolling in over the mountains. Soon his headlights would do him no good. Besides being crippled, he'd be as good as blind in the pea-soup fog.

Chapter Fourteen

Slowing the Austin to a safer speed as thick portions of the fog bank obscured sections of the road, Brian peered into the mist. In her red shirt and dark jeans, Molly would be practically invisible at night under the best of circumstances. The only comforting thing about that thought was the fact that if he couldn't see her, neither could anyone up to no good.

Brian slammed his fist against the steering wheel and cursed. How long had she been gone? Could she have gotten this far, or had he passed her already? He'd been so introspective right after she'd left his bed, he wasn't sure how long he'd lain there before deciding to get dressed and follow her.

He shivered. Dressed, did he say? Without a shirt or jacket, he was damned cold. The convertible offered almost no protection, either, and within the fog bank, the night air held an even greater chill than usual.

The idea of turning back flitted through his mind and was summarily dismissed without consideration. The only way he'd quit was when and if he found Molly. Until then, he didn't care if he froze to death.

Dropping down out of the hills onto Valley Parkway, he was pleased to see that he'd outrun the encroaching fog. Once it crossed the ridge it would spill over into the valley and blanket Escondido, too, but as yet it hadn't come that far.

He shifted gears. At least this area was lighted. Looking around, he noticed to his chagrin that although there were shops, gas stations and the usual other amenities of civilization, almost everything was closed due to the late hour. Brian's jaw clenched. Molly was no safer here than she'd been in the hills. And she was nowhere in sight.

Turning onto her street, he drew a shuddering breath, his hands gripping the wheel till his knuckles were white, his heart so thankful he thought it would burst. There she was! Back straight, pride evident, she was practically stamping her feet with each step. And she was almost home.

He cruised up behind her and slowed to a crawl. She ignored the presence of the car and kept her eyes straight ahead.

"Pardon me?" Brian called. Molly made no reply, but he did see her start, and he sensed an added stiffness in her demeanor.

"Excuse me!" He honked. "Hey, I said excuse me."

She whirled. "There is no excuse for you. What do you . . . ?" Wide-eyed, she peered into the car, then exhaled noisily. "Good grief. I thought you were naked."

"I almost am. And I'm freezing," he countered.

"Then go home."

"No. Not until you agree to marry me."

She began walking again, noting out of the corner of her eye that he was driving along at the same pace. "I'm never getting married. I told you that."

"Why?"

"Because I don't believe in marriage. I told you that, too."

Desperate, Brian wished she'd at least get into the car so he could stop shouting. When he asked her to, she refused, leaving him no choice but to say what was on his mind for the whole world to hear.

"Remember what I told you about working on your van?" he called, taking a slightly different approach.

Molly hesitated. "What does my van have to do with this?"

"I was scared to try to fix it for fear I'd fail, because then I'd be *sure* I couldn't do it." He paused. "I felt that way in bed, too, if you must know."

Beginning to weaken, she still wasn't convinced. "So?"

"So the same thing is wrong with you."

Molly was not about to begin discussing being in bed with Brian while standing in the middle of the street where all her neighbors could listen. She did, however, yearn to hear more. Searching her memory for a pertinent quip, she finally decided to focus on his mention of her van.

"You're telling me I need new spark plugs and a fuel pump?" she asked.

Relieved to hear her making a joke, Brian began to relax a little. Loosening his grip on the wheel, he flexed his aching fingers, one hand at a time. "You need a new point of view."

"Such as?" Stopping and turning toward him, she stood with her hands on her hips.

"Marry me. Try it. I'll bet our love lasts forever."

Rolling her eyes, she started to walk away again. "There is no forever."

Brian gave the car a little gas. "Okay. Then how about ten years? Just ten. That's all I ask."

"No."

"Five?"

"No!"

"A week and a half. Tops."

Molly fought the smile that kept wanting to lift the corners of her mouth. If she could be happy with anyone, anytime, anywhere, it would be Brian. It always had been. "You're nuts, Forrester. Nobody gets married for only a week and a half."

"*Now* you're getting it." He saw her smile erupt like a sunrise, and he held his breath as she shook her head in apparent resignation and took a few tentative steps toward the car.

"Well, you're *not* getting 'it,' as you once told me," Molly warned.

As she drew closer, Brian's heart raced out of control. Oh, God, was she really coming to him? Afraid to breathe, he waited, praying she was.

Molly lowered her voice. "I don't care if it takes us months to figure out how to make love, you are going to marry me first. Got that?"

She'd reached the car. Brian leaned over, opened the door for her and held out his arms. Molly fell into his embrace, wrapping her arms around him.

"There are books we could read if we have trouble," Brian said between rapid, hungry kisses. "Oh, Molly, I love you so. Don't be angry at me for putting you off. I was afraid I couldn't be the man you needed and like a fool, I used the first excuse that came to mind. If that hadn't worked, I'd have found something else."

She drew her palm slowly along his cheek, caressing it, and looked into the eyes of love. "We don't need sex manuals, and you know it, Mr. Forrester. All we need is each other."

"That's all we've ever needed," he said, kissing her tenderly, breathlessly. "Our problem has always been the old pain and past problems we were both unwilling to let go of."

"I'm still afraid to promise you forever," Molly told him.

"I've been taking life a day at a time since I was hurt," Brian whispered. "And each day with you will be a doubly exciting miracle. We'll make it, Molly. I know we will."

Settling against his chest, she ran her hands over the chilled flesh, kissed him and leaned away. It was important to look at him when she said, "I believe you. I love you, Brian Forrester. Make me your wife."

Epilogue

The church pews were filled to overflowing. Those wedding guests in wheelchairs who wouldn't fit along the side aisles were lined up in the back of the room. Molly hadn't counted, but she bet there were at least twenty companion dogs present, too. Little Sam, the corgi, sat on a bench beside his new mistress while she and a friend signed to each other in silent conversation, waiting for the ceremony to begin.

Bev straightened Molly's veil. "You look beautiful."

"Thanks." Molly smoothed her simple, princess-style, white satin gown, remembering fondly the silk teddy she wore beneath it. "I hope Brian isn't disappointed."

"No way!" Smiling broadly, Bev winked at her. "You never did tell me what it's like . . . making love with him, I mean."

Molly blushed. "No, and I never will. Besides, we haven't . . . you know."

"Why not? Good grief, if you were buying a used car, you'd test drive it first."

"Cute," Molly said. "But not for me. If

Brian and I had gone ahead and made love, he'd always wonder if I'd have married him only if he'd pleased me in bed. I couldn't do that to him. I love him too much."

"Wow. I hope I find somebody who cares about me like that someday."

"You will. And when you do, don't be afraid to love him back." Molly picked up her bouquet of roses and baby's breath. "Is Brian's brother in place yet?"

Bev peeked out. "Uh-huh. And here comes Brian, right behind him. Boy, he looks handsome! You ready?"

Molly swallowed hard and nodded. "Get the basket of rose petals for me, will you? I'm so nervous, I'd probably spill them."

"You're sure this will work?"

"We rehearsed it. If Brian remembers to give the proper signals, Fremont should be fine." Bending over, Molly held out the basket of flower petals Bev had given her, and the obedient Lab took the handle in his mouth. His FFI backpack had been decorated with shasta daisies and white satin ribbons for the occasion, and his ebony coat gleamed.

The organ music swelled, shooting happy chills up Molly's spine. It was now or never. No one in her family had come forth to give the bride away, but it no longer mattered to Molly. She was going down that aisle to her

242

Brian. That was all that counted. "Okay, Bev. Get ready. You follow the . . . flower girl."

Molly motioned to Fremont. He was supposed to go part way to the altar, pause and shake himself, thereby scattering rose petals on the floor. She watched him step tentatively through the door, stop and look around at all the people. No one moved, least of all Fremont.

"Go," Molly urged. "Go find Brian."

Fremont stood stock-still, the handle of the flower basket clamped securely in his teeth.

"Here, Fremont," Brian called loudly. "It's okay, boy. I'm here."

With a happy wag of his tail, the excited dog began a headlong gallop, bounding down the center aisle of the church amid laughter and applause. In his wake he left every rose petal the basket had contained raining down on the crowd.

Molly laughed, knowing just how Fremont felt. If she hadn't been hampered by her long, white gown and the expected formality of the occasion, she'd have run to Brian the same way. She could hardly wait!

The employees of THORNDIKE PRESS hope you have enjoyed this Large Print book. All our Large Print books are designed for easy reading — and they're made to last.

Other Thorndike Large Print books are available at your library, through selected bookstores, or directly from us. Suggestions for books you would like to see in Large Print are always welcome.

For more information about current and upcoming titles, please call or mail your name and address to:

THORNDIKE PRESS
PO Box 159
Thorndike, Maine 04986
800/223-6121
207/948-2962